# BIGGLES TAKES A HAND

'If you will go to the Adlon Restaurant in
Bank Street, Kensington, today at a quarter
to one precisely, and sit at table number
two, you will be joined by someone who will
give you information you should be glad
to have. A Well-wisher.'
'You can't come to much harm in
Kensington,' said Bertie. But the anonymous
letter set Biggles off on a trail of espionage
and murder that took him to Berlin.

CAPTAIN W. E. JOHNS

---

# BIGGLES TAKES
# A HAND

KNIGHT BOOKS
*the paperback division of Brockhampton Press*

ISBN 0 340 19088 4

*This edition first published 1975 by Knight,
the paperback division of Brockhampton Press, Leicester.
First published in 1963 by Hodder & Stoughton Ltd*

*Text copyright © 1963 Capt. W. E. Johns*

*Printed and bound in Great Britain by
Cox & Wyman Ltd,
London, Reading and Fakenham*

# CONTENTS

# CHAPTER 1

# A SINISTER
# ASSIGNATION

---

'LETTER for you.' Ginger handed it to Biggles who, in his dressing-gown, at home in the London flat, was sipping an early morning cup of tea with the first cigarette of the day.

Biggles looked at the envelope, back and front. 'This didn't come through the post. There's no stamp and no address; just my name. Where did you find it?'

'In our box, when I went down for the papers. Somebody must have dropped it in during the night.'

'It isn't often I get a letter here,' remarked Biggles, as he slit the flap. 'I can't recall ever seeing this handwriting before, either.' He withdrew the single sheet of notepaper contained in the envelope and read what was written on it. He took a sip of tea and read it again.

'Come on, old boy; what's it all about,' inquired Bertie, from the other side of the table. 'You're killing me with curiosity.'

Said Algy, softly: 'From his expression somebody's trying to touch him for some money.'

Biggles looked up. 'You're right off the beam. Listen

to this.' He read aloud: ' "If you will go to the Adlon Restaurant in Bank Street, Kensington, today, at a quarter to one precisely, and sit at table number two, you will be joined by someone who will give you information you should be glad to have. A Well-wisher." ' He tossed the letter on the table. 'What do you make of that?'

Ginger answered. 'Only what it says. Are you going to keep the appointment?'

'That needs thinking about.'

'There is this about it,' asserted Bertie, cheerfully. 'You can't come to much harm in Kensington.'

'I wasn't contemplating any such possibility,' returned Biggles. 'I'm not alarmed, if that's what you're thinking. It's the man who wrote this letter who is scared. It's just that I don't like anonymous letters.'

'What makes you think he's scared?'

'What other reason could there be for his reluctance to divulge his identity? That doesn't necessarily mean that he's frightened physically; but he must be mighty anxious that no one should know what he's doing.'

'Some crook who's lost his nerve and is prepared to squeal, perhaps,' suggested Ginger.

Biggles shook his head. 'I don't think that's the answer. If I know anything about crooks such a man would have got in touch with Scotland Yard; probably by phoning from a call-box. Why pick on me, personally? Obviously the writer knows me and knows what I do for a living. He knew I lived here. How? I've taken good care to keep my private address under the hat. Our number isn't in the phone book. I kept it out. No doubt the man who wrote this letter would have preferred to phone had he known the number. I feel I should keep the appointment if for no other reason than to find out how the fellow got this address. I don't like that.'

'Will you go alone?' put in Algy.

'I see nothing in the invitation about bringing a guest so I shall have to go alone.'

'Then you've decided to go?'

'I might as well. I've nothing to lose.' Biggles smiled. 'On the contrary, if my unknown well-wisher turns out to be a man with money in his pocket I might get a free lunch. Let's leave it at that. I'd better be getting dressed.' Biggles stubbed his cigarette, finished his tea and retired to his bedroom.

He arrived at the rendezvous five minutes early, thinking that, as he had never heard of the place, he might have some difficulty in finding it. It did in fact take him a little while, and when he saw it he understood why the name was unknown to him. It was small, and while not exactly shabby it did not give the impression of being prosperous. In a word, it was like thousands of similar eating establishments to be found in and around the metropolis which somehow manage to make a living for the proprietors.

However, when Biggles went in he found the place fairly well patronised, from which it could be assumed that the food served was reasonably good. This became understandable when presently he picked up a menu card and observed that the various dishes offered were not as cheap as he had expected they would be. In short, the dining-room was far from being in the 'sausage and mash' class which he had suspected from the outside. The important thing, from his point of view, was that the table-cloths and cutlery were clean.

He counted fourteen tables, laid for parties of from two to four, fairly well spaced along a room that was

long and rather narrow. A waitress came forward and
asked him if he had booked a table. He said he was to
meet a friend at table number two, whereupon the girl
escorted him the full length of the room to a table laid
for two and pulled out a chair which, either by accident
or design, commanded a view of every other table in the
restaurant. It occurred to him to wonder if this had been
arranged, but he thought it prudent not to inquire. He
was inclined to think it had, because his host would have
his back to the room, which was in accord with the
surreptitious nature of the proceedings.

People continued to trickle in and sit down. In particular he noticed a party of three, because from the
confident way they entered, and went straight to a table
without waiting for the waitress, they were evidently
regulars. He did not pay any further attention to them,
however, assuming his host, when he arrived, would be
alone.

At a quarter to one the first man who had entered by
himself walked in. He, too, behaved as though he knew
his way about, giving a nod to the waitress in passing
her. He was thin, and tall above the average, but as the
lower part of his face was hidden by a grey beard, and
the upper part by dark glasses, little of his features
could be seen. Walking with a slight limp he came
straight on to the table where Biggles was seated and sat
in the opposite chair.

'I'm glad you could come, Bigglesworth,' he said
softly.

Biggles stared, frowning. He still did not recognise
the man from his appearance but he knew the voice.
'Von Stalhein,' he breathed, incredulously. 'So it's you!
What's the idea of this theatrical stuff?'

'Ssh. No names. And please speak quietly. This

happens to be one of those occasions when a disguise is very necessary.'

'For heaven's sake! Why?'

'Because there are men in the room I would not like to recognise me.'

'You know them?'

'Yes. And they know me.'

'Did you know they would be here?'

'I reckoned on it.'

'Then if you didn't want them to see you why in the name of common sense did you come here?'

'Because I wanted you to see them. To have a good look at them, so that you will know them again where-ever you might meet them. Here you have ample time to study them, which would not be easy outside in the street.'

'Which men are you talking about?'

'There are three of them. They are sitting at the far end of the room near the door that leads into the kitchen. One is going bald in front.'

Biggles nodded. 'I've got them. I noticed them when they came in.'

'Why?'

'Because from their behaviour I took them to be regulars.'

'They have had their lunch here every day for at least a week. It so happens that I often use this restaurant. The food is quite good and within reach of my purse. I assumed they would be here again today, which is why I sent you the invitation to join me.'

'Have you been watching them?'

'Not seriously. I have other things to do. But knowing who and what they are I found myself wondering what they are doing in England. There is a chance they are looking for me, but I don't think so. I am no longer a man of importance, or of sufficient importance to warrant their employment. Still, one never knows. The day I came in and saw them sitting there I turned about and went out. Fortunately they did not see me. Since then I have thought it advisable to alter my appearance. When such people are about one cannot be too careful.'

'I see. Now perhaps you'll tell me how I come into the picture.'

'After giving the matter careful thought I decided that, in return for the political asylum I have received here, someone in authority should know who these men are and why they have come here. There can be only one reason. Naturally, I thought of you.'

'Very well. Who are these men?'

'They are probably three of the most dangerous men in the world.'

'Very interesting. In what respect?'

'They are professional murderers'

Biggles frowned. 'Say that again.'

'I said their chosen job in life is assassination, in which unpleasant trade they are experts, having had a good deal of experience. To put it plainly, those three villains are in the employment of men who from time to time decide that someone, for one reason or another, must be killed to ensure his silence. There are not many people in the world who find it necessary to employ killers, so no doubt you will guess to whom I am referring. As you see, the three agents are in England. That can only mean they have been sent here to destroy someone. They are not criminals in the common meaning of the word. I am speaking only of political murder, although no doubt for a consideration they would undertake to liquidate anyone.'

Biggles looked hard at Von Stalhein's face. 'Had anyone else told me that I would have had doubts; but knowing you as I do I am sure you wouldn't waste my time, or your own, fabricating such a monstrous story.'

At this point the conversation was interrupted by the arrival of the waitress, notebook in hand, for their order. They both decided on steak and fried potatoes with half a pint of beer.

While this was going on Biggles took the opportunity to study the faces of the three men Von Stalhein had brought him to the restaurant to see.

On close scrutiny one could only say that they did not look British, although the reason for this was not immediately apparent. It may have been the clothes they wore, and the materials used, for there is something about the cut of an English-made suit that is different from others. Generally speaking there was nothing about any of them to indicate what Von Stalhein had claimed to be their sinister occupation.

The man with the half-bald head had a rather square face, clean shaven. His eyes were set wide apart and there was a grim set to his jaw, although in the ordinary way this would not have been noticed. His movements were slow and deliberate. Another of the trio was almost his exact opposite, being lean, with deep-set eyes that were never still under straight black eyebrows that met above the nose. He had a thick crop of hair without a parting. The third member was as conventional a type as could be met anywhere. His face was pale, his mouth wide with lips thin and bloodless. He looked as if he might have been ill. He kept a cigarette going through the meal and coughed frequently.

The waitress having departed Biggles turned his eyes

back to Von Stalhein. 'How do you know about these men?'

A ghost of a smile for a second softened Von Stalhein's customary austere expression. 'Let us not go into my past history. Let it suffice that I have known of these men for some long time. I have never associated with them, but I was once asked to assist them. This, being a soldier and not a murderer, I refused, with the result that I knew would be inevitable. As you know, in certain countries the refusal to obey an order involves a trial on a charge of treason. This, as a matter of detail, was the reason why I was condemned to life imprisonment on the island of Sakhalin, from which vile durance you so kindly rescued me.'*

'Who was to be murdered on that occasion?' inquired Biggles.

'You.'

Biggles smiled whimsically. 'As a matter of fact an attempt on my life was made about that time, but it misfired. A man fired a gun at me from inside a car as I was walking home. But to return to the present: have I ever run up against these particular men, without being aware of their identity?'

'Not to my knowledge. They are not engaged in espionage, or anything of that nature. Their job is to liquidate any person named by their employers. They can employ any method they wish.'

'I've sometimes made myself a nuisance to people we both know,' said Biggles thoughtfully. 'Could it be that these cold-blooded gentlemen are here to get *me*?'

'I've considered that possibility. I would hardly think so. If I may presume to say so I doubt if you are now sufficiently important. These men are only employed

* See *Biggles Buries the Hatchet.*

when someone who could cause mischief is to be, to use the popular expression, bumped off. Besides, had you been the target, as they have been in the country for at least a week it is unlikely that neither you nor they would be sitting here now. They would be on their way home, their mission accomplished.'

'That at least is a comforting thought,' rejoined Biggles cheerfully. 'What are the names of these thugs?'

'I imagine they have many, with passports for all of them. When I knew them, the name of the leader – he's the man with the bald head – was Ludwig Karkoff. He's the planner. The other two are his assistants. They are the actual executioners. Their names are Molsk – on the left as you look at them – and Rallensky.'

'What nationality are they?'

'I don't know. They may not know themselves. I know they speak many languages, one of the accomplishments that makes them so useful. They belong to what we might call the international brigade. As a result of the war, when so many people were displaced, Eastern Europe is full of such men.'

'Why have these vultures never been caught at their dirty trade?'

'They have an advantage denied ordinary criminals. If hard pressed they can always find refuge in one of the Iron Curtain embassies, not only in London but in any country in Western Europe. That gives them diplomatic immunity while arrangements are being made to send them home. It is all too easy.'

At this juncture there was another delay while the waitress served their food.

Then Biggles went on: 'Assuming these men are living in London do you happen to know where they are staying?'

'Yes, I can tell you that. Anticipating your question I have made a point of watching them go home. I think they must have rooms in one of the many private hotels in the Cromwell Road. It is called the Cosmolite, one that appears to cater particularly for foreigners – as the name would suggest. Of course, I know what you are going to say about all this.'

'What am I going to say?'

'You will say there is nothing you can do about it.'

Biggles shrugged. 'As this is a free country no man can be arrested until he has broken the law.'

'Not even if, as in this case, you know what he intends to do?'

'How can you prove what a man intends to do until he has done it?'

Von Stalhein shook his head sadly. 'That, if I may presume to say so, is the weakness of a democracy.'

'Let's not get on to politics,' requested Biggles. 'We have ways and means of dealing with special circumstances.'

'Such as?'

'If we could prove that these men had entered the country by using false papers we could get a deportation order.'

'Even if you did that it wouldn't solve your big problem. They would merely be replaced by others. In fact, you would have done yourself a disservice. It is better to deal with men you know than those you don't know.'

Biggles agreed. 'Our real problem is to find out why these men are here. In plain English, who they have come here to murder? Have you any idea of the probable victim?'

'No. Why should I?'

'I imagine you read the newspapers so it struck me you might know the names of some of the people here who are not popular with the various dictators and their puppets.'

'The person who has been sentenced to death may not be in this country at the moment. He may be coming here. Look at it like this. The murderers have been here for a week or more. Why haven't they struck? I can think of only two reasons. Either the proposed victim is not here or they have been unable to locate him.'

'I take your point,' said Biggles slowly. 'If we knew the name of the man we should be able to judge the reason for killing him. There could be several. If he happened to be a foreign diplomat his assassination in this country could have tremendous repercussions. Fanned by propaganda it could turn friendly countries into enemies, and that could have more far-reaching effects in the world, as it is today, than the death of the man himself. Do you know the method usually employed by these professional murderers?'

'No. I only know that whenever possible the death is made to look like an accident. For example, the man might fall off a boat and be drowned. He might fall out of a window to crash on the pavement below. That has happened. The aeroplane in which he is to travel could be sabotaged.'

'And kill a lot of innocent people at the same time.'

'You don't suppose that would worry them,' sneered Von Stalhein.

'I see they're getting ready to move off,' said Biggles, looking up the room at the three men under discussion.

'I must go, too,' said Von Stalhein, beckoning to the waitress for the bill. 'I have work to do.'

'I'm very much obliged to you for what you've told me,' thanked Biggles seriously. 'Also for an excellent lunch.'

'Don't mention it. I'm glad to be of service and it has been a pleasure to see you again.'

Biggles smiled broadly. 'There was a time when you wouldn't have said that.'

Von Stalhein remained serious. 'Times change, and as we grow older, if we are wise we change with them. But before we part there is one thing I must ask you. Tell no one except your worthy assistants, who I know are to be trusted, of this meeting, or of the purpose of it.'

Biggles hesitated. 'If I am to follow this up I'm bound to tell my chief. He, too, is to be trusted.'

'I must leave that to your discretion, but I see no reason why you should mention my name unless it becomes absolutely imperative.'

'What's your objection?'

'If you tell Air Commodore Raymond he may tell the Chief Commissioner; he would tell your security people; they might have to tell your Home Secretary, or Foreign Secretary; and so it could go on until the story reached the newspapers. Then all the world would know. I am trying to lead a quiet life, but once my name was mentioned that would end abruptly.'

Biggles finished his beer and lit a cigarette. 'You can rely on me to do my utmost to see that doesn't happen.'

'Thank you.'

'Are you still at the same address in case I should want to get in touch with you?'

'Yes. I still get quite a lot of work, chiefly translations, from one of your government departments, and that is why, being grateful, I am glad to be of assistance whenever possible.'

'Good. Then let's leave it at that.' Biggles held out a hand. 'Good-bye for now. You go out first. I'll follow you in a minute.'

They shook hands and parted, Von Stalhein limping slowly to the door.

Biggles, with a curious expression on his face, watched him go. He gave him two or three minutes and followed him out into the street.

CHAPTER 2

# DEAD END?

WHEN Biggles left the Adlon Restaurant he walked to the High Street, called a taxi and went straight to Scotland Yard. In his office he found his assistants waiting with some impatience for the explanation of the mysterious letter. This they had to contain, for all Biggles said as he hung up his cap and walked to the intercom. telephone on his desk was this: 'I'll talk to you presently. I shall have to speak to the Chief right away, if he's in.' He pressed the appropriate button.

'Bigglesworth here, sir,' he said. 'May I have a word with you? Yes, sir, it's urgent. Good. I'm on my way down.' As he made for the door he said briefly to the others: 'I'll be back.'

In the Air Commodore's office he began without preamble. 'Is there, to your knowledge, anyone in this country whose death would be a desirable event for a hostile power?'

The Air Commodore sat back, his eyes slowly opening wide. 'What an extraordinary question!'

'Let's put it another way. Is there anyone here, or on his way here, possibly an important figure in world politics, whose assassination would embarrass the British Government?'

The Air Commodore studied Biggles' face carefully

before he answered. 'I couldn't say offhand. You must have a very good reason for such a question. May I know what it is?'

'I expected you to ask that and obviously I can't decline to give you an answer. It is this. There has arrived in this country a party of three mercenary killers whose job it is to liquidate persons named by those who employ them.'

'You mean – political murders.'

'I have no definite information about that but I imagine so.'

'How do you know these men are here?'

'I've seen them.'

'When?'

'About an hour ago.'

'Do you know their names?'

'I do – unless they are working under assumed ones while on their mission to England.'

'As you know so much you might also know where they are living.'

'Yes, I know that, too.'

'You *have* been busy.'

'No, sir. The information came to me through a friend.'

'You're sure this is not a cock-and-bull story?'

'Quite sure. The man who put me on the trail doesn't invent things, or imagine them. He's too busy to waste his time, or mine.'

'I see you take this matter seriously.'

'Don't you?'

'I'd like to know more about it before I commit myself.'

'While we're waiting for that the mischief might be done. Should that happen there would be no point in doing anything. You wouldn't even get the murderers.'

'Why not?'

'Because they would be secure under cover of diplomatic immunity.'

The Air Commodore frowned. 'Really, Bigglesworth, you're beginning to alarm me.'

'I came here prepared for that. I would have been disappointed had I failed to do so.'

'Very well. What do you suggest I do about it?'

'Provide the answer to my original question. You should be able to get it. I can't. Until we know who it is these people are after we shall be working in the dark.'

The Air Commodore considered the problem. 'You know, Bigglesworth, this doesn't really come within our province.'

'I realise that, but I'm afraid it will have to if precautions are to be taken.'

'Why?'

'Because if you pass this on to another department it'll be all over bar the shouting. The enemy will know what's going on and go to ground.'

'Are you suggesting that our security people are in the habit of talking carelessly?'

'I wouldn't know about that; but what I do know, and you know as well as I do, is that the people behind this murder outfit have spies everywhere. I repeat, *everywhere*. Wherefore I say the fewer the people who know what's in the wind the less will be the chance of a friend of this country being murdered. Not only the man himself. A lot of innocent people might die with him.'

'How?'

'In a sabotaged aircraft, which is one of the methods

employed by our visitors to make murder look like an accident.' Biggles lit a cigarette. 'That's all, sir. I've told you what I know so from now on you carry the responsibility.'

'All right – all right. There's no need to get hot under the collar about it. You've sprung this thing on me out of the blue. You can't expect me to give you an answer in five minutes. It needs serious thought.'

'Fair enough, sir; but don't think too long. There isn't much I can do in the meantime but I shall be thinking, too.'

'You won't tell me the name of the man from whom you got this information?'

'For a moment I'd rather not.'

'Why?'

'Because he has a very good reason for not wanting to be involved. If it were known that he had taken me into his confidence the chances are that his name would also go on the murder list.'

The Air Commodore agreed that was a good enough reason.

'He has told me as much as he knows, and went to some trouble to do it,' went on Biggles. 'What he doesn't know, and I wouldn't expect him to know, is the name of the person due to be liquidated. It may be someone who is already in this country, but more likely, I think, to be someone on his way here, or booked to come here in the near future.'

'Why don't you think it might be someone already here?'

'Had that been the case I imagine he would be dead by now, and the killers on their way home. They've been here for at least a week, and they are still here. As I see it they are either waiting for someone or have so far failed

to find out where he is. Either way one thing is certain.
They know who it is they've been ordered to get. If they
know, surely there must be someone in this country,
probably in a government department, who could put a
finger on the most likely candidate for political execution. After all, it must be someone pretty high up, or
those who want him out of the way wouldn't go to such
lengths as they obviously have.'

'Yes,' murmured the Air Commodore pensively. 'I
can see that. You'd better leave this with me for the time
being. I'll start making inquiries right away and let you
know at once if I get results.'

'Okay, sir. We'll leave it at that. ' Biggles got up and
left the room.

'What the devil's going on?' greeted Algy wonder-
ingly, as Biggles re-entered his own office.

'Keep quiet and I'll tell you,' replied Biggles, crossing
to his desk and dropping into the chair.

'Did you discover who wrote that bally letter? That's
what I want to know,' asked Bertie, impatiently.

'I did.'

'Someone we know?'

'Yes. But don't start guessing because you wouldn't
get it in a month of Sundays.'

'Tell us. I can't wait,' pleaded Ginger.

'Von Stalhein.'

Silence fell, everyone staring.

'Has he gone round the bend?' queried Algy.

'No. He seemed perfectly normal except in his appearance, the result of sticking a set of false whiskers on
his face. That wasn't for fun. He had a good reason for
not wanting to be recognised by another party in the
restaurant. And now, if you'll listen instead of firing
questions at me I'll tell you what it was all about. But

mark this. Not a word of what I'm going to say must go outside this room.'

Thereupon Biggles related the story of his meeting with Von Stalhein and the purpose of it. 'Now you'll understand why I couldn't get to the Chief fast enough when I came in.'

'What had he to say about it?' inquired Algy.

'Not much. I hoped he'd be able to tell me right away the name of the person booked for the high jump; but he couldn't.'

'Wasn't he worried?'

'Not particularly. But I think he will be when what I told him has had time to soak in.'

'What's he doing about it?'

'The only thing he can do at the moment is try to find out who it is these unpleasant visitors are here to murder. Anyway, that's what I asked him to do.'

'And what are we going to do?'

'Frankly, I don't know. I can't see how we can do much without more information.'

Bertie gave his opinion. 'The obvious thing to do is round up these three stiffs, tie some bricks to their feet and pitch 'em into the nearest river.'

'I couldn't agree more,' answered Biggles. 'That would be doing mankind a real service. Unfortunately the laws of this land disapprove of that sort of remedy. What pains me in this particular case is, if these merciless hounds do commit murder they'll probably get away with it by taking cover in a convenient foreign embassy. No doubt all that sort of thing is carefully arranged. It seems silly, but it boils down to this. We can't touch them till they've done their monstrous work and then we shouldn't be able to get at them.'

'Silly?' scoffed Bertie. 'I'd call it crazy.'

Algy spoke. 'Suppose the Air Commodore learns the name of the probable victim, surely he'd be warned of what might happen?'

'A nice embarrassing situation that would cause. You invite a friend to visit you and then have to say to him, "Sorry, but as a result of your coming here you've displeased certain people who have decided to have you murdered." You'd have to be pretty thick-skinned to drop a clanger like that.'

'He could ask for police protection,' said Ginger.

'I imagine he'd get that anyway – that is, if he's of sufficient importance to have a murder gang laid on to silence him for good. The murderers will have taken all that into account and make their plans accordingly. But it's no use guessing. That won't get us anywhere. Before we can take preventative measures we've got to know the name of the man being stalked by these professional assassins, where he is and where he's likely to be in the near future. That might give us a lead as to how and when these murdering swine plan to get at him. I can't recall seeing in the newspapers the name of any VIP in this country now, or on his way here.'

'People are always coming and going,' Algy pointed out. 'How could you possibly say which is the one they're after?'

'Somebody should know. The nature of his visit to this country should provide a clue.'

'Even so, I don't see how knowing his name is going to help us,' argued Algy. 'You still wouldn't be able to touch the villains until they'd struck. Why us, anyhow. This sort of thing isn't up our street. Surely it's a job for the Security people.'

'There are reasons, one being that bar Von Stalhein I'm the only man in this country able to recognise the members of the murder gang. For another, there may be an attempt to sabotage an aircraft. The Security people may take over later. I argued this point with the Air Commodore. It doesn't need me to tell you that there are more spies in this country – and every other country for that matter – than ever before. They get into the highest places. If word leaked out that we're wise to what's going on our difficulties would be doubled. So the fewer the people in the know the better.'

Ginger stepped in. 'The man who's been condemned to death may not be a visitor from overseas. How do you know he's not British and a resident of this country?'

'I don't know. I can only assume. The killer agents have been here for at least a week. Why haven't they struck? Why the delay? If the proposed victim lives in this country they'd have known where to find him when they arrived. Their plans would have been prearranged. By now they would have done their job and be on their way home. The fact that they are still here can only mean the victim isn't dead yet. So I can only think they're waiting for him to arrive.'

'Well, what are you going to do?' asked Algy. 'Wait till you hear from the Air Commodore?'

Biggles lit a cigarette. 'I don't like the idea of wasting time, every hour of which might be valuable. There's one obvious thing we must do. At present I'm the only one who knows these murderers by sight. That's something you should all know and I can't see any difficulty about it. Tomorrow when I go back to the Adlon Restaurant for lunch to check if the killers are still about, I'll take you with me. I'll book a table for four. That should give you all a chance to have a good look at them; but don't stare. Men in their line of business notice little things.'

'What if they don't turn up?' asked Algy.

'In that case the next step would be to find out if they're still at their hotel in the Cromwell Road. Unless I have news from the Air Commodore we'll leave it at that.'

This settled Biggles busied himself in the office on various jobs for the rest of the day, not daring to leave for fear a call came through from the Air Commodore to give him the information he so urgently needed. The others stayed with him.

Seven o'clock came, and he had nearly given up hope when the call came through for him to go down, and keen with expectation he hastened to obey.

The Chief greeted him with a peculiar smile. 'I can put your mind at rest,' he began.

Biggles looked puzzled. 'In what way?'

'I'm afraid your informant was either pulling your leg or talking through his hat.'

'Why, what do you mean?' replied Biggles, taken aback.

'As far as we – that is, the Government – are concerned, there is no one in this country at present, or on his way here, whose assassination would have the slightest effect on current political affairs.'

Biggles looked amazed. 'There must be some mistake, sir.'

The Commodore lifted a shoulder. 'The Special Branch* should know. They've had no orders to guard or keep a particular eye on anyone.'

'I must admit they should know,' agreed Biggles. 'But I can't help feeling there's something wrong somewhere. Three professional killers are in the country.

---

* The Special Branch at Scotland Yard is concerned with national security and the protection of public personages from harm.

There's no doubt whatever about that. I've seen them.'

'How do you know they're killers?'

'I was told by a man who has every reason to know. Are we to believe they've merely come here for a holiday?'

'You can work that out as you like. I've given you the information you asked for. There's no one here who matters two hoots so you might as well forget about it.'

'I see. Thank you, sir. I'm sorry I troubled you.' With that Biggles left the room and returned to his office.

'Well, who's been put on the spot,' inquired Ginger.

'Apparently no one. It seems there's no one here worth putting on the spot.'

'I don't get it.'

'That's the surprise packet the Chief has just handed to me. He says there's no one here, or on his way here, whose death would cause us the slightest concern. The Special Branch haven't received orders to stand by.'

'What did you say to that?'

'What could I say? I was in no position to argue.'

'Do you believe it?'

'They believe it. As far as I'm concerned I don't know what to believe. On the one hand the Chief should know what he's talking about; on the other, Von Stalhein is equally well informed – in some matters maybe better. One thing is certain. Three men employed in political murders are in London. Of that there can be no doubt whatever. Von Stalhein knows them by sight. He knows their names. Had it been one man it might possibly be a case of mistaken identity. But not three together. That would be too much of a coincidence. Von Stalhein never had the slightest doubt, so I'm bound to accept it as a fact that they're here. Why did they come? Why are they still here? Don't ask me to believe they've come to see the sights. It's unlikely they'd be allowed to leave their base, wherever that might be, unless they'd been given a definite mission.' Biggles lit a cigarette.

'Then you're still convinced that Von Stalhein is right all along the line,' put in Bertie.

'I am.'

'Then what does it all add up to, in view of what the Chief has just told you?'

'I can arrive at only one possible conclusion. There is someone in this country, or on his way here, about whom the authorities know nothing. What I mean is, the person might be known to them by name, but his movements are not known.'

'Would it be possible for such a person to creep into the country under the curtain – if you see what I mean,' queried Bertie.

'These murdering thugs have obviously been able to get in.'

'So what do we do?' asked Algy. 'Forget about it?'

'Not on your life. Not yet, anyway. It'd be on my conscience if some poor devil was bumped off when I might have been able to prevent it. I shall carry on in my own way till something happens to turn the spotlight on the mystery.'

'Then do I take it that tomorrow's arrangement still stands?'

'Definitely. But let's pack up. It's getting late. A bite of something to eat may help to get the old brain-box functioning.'

# CHAPTER 3

# VON STALHEIN GIVES
# A HINT

THE following day, at a little before twelve-thirty, they were all in Kensington, walking briskly towards the Adlon Restaurant, Biggles having resolved to arrive early to be sure of getting a table. He had already described the men so that the others would know each one by name as he entered, assuming of course that they came.

'This is the place,' he said, as they stopped outside. 'Remember the drill. Don't stare at them. One good look as they sit down should be enough to get their faces photographed on your minds. If we can get a table near them we might recognise the language they use. It's unlikely they'll talk in English, but there's just a chance we might catch a name if one occurs in the conversation. When they leave, I want you, Ginger, to tail them and see where they go.'

'Suppose they don't all leave together?'

'In that case you'll follow the first to leave. Algy will follow the second party if it breaks up. That's about all we can do. As far as we ourselves are concerned there must be no mention of what we're doing. Men like these develop sharp ears. Stick to trivialities – football, cricket, anything you like. Okay. Let's go in.'

Only a few customers had arrived and they were at the far end of the room. The same waitress was on duty. It so happened that the table next to the one in which they were interested was laid for four, and unoccupied. Biggles asked the girl if they could have it. She said it had not been reserved so they took it.

To Biggles' satisfaction, and somewhat to his surprise, no sooner had they sat down and ordered their meal, taking the full course luncheon to cover as much time as possible, than the men they had come to observe walked in. Their manner was alert, as if they were in a hurry, which, Biggles reasoned, accounted for their arrival earlier than usual. The impression of haste was confirmed by the way Karkoff, after a glance at his watch, called the waitress. He gave his order to the girl in English with a strong foreign accent tinged with an American twang, as if he might have learned the language in that country although he was obviously not a native either of the United States or Canada. Thereafter he spoke with his companions, in a voice low but just audible, in a tongue which Biggles was unable to recognise. This was to be expected, for men of the same nationality, wherever they might be, usually carry on their conversation in the language in which they are most familiar, normally their mother tongue.

Thereafter the meal proceeded in the customary manner. Although snatches of conversation could be overheard Biggles learned nothing from those at the next table. From time to time Karkoff looked at his watch. At length he said something sharply, whereupon Rallensky got up and leaving the others to pay the bill went out.

Ginger finished his coffee and with a casual 'See you later,' also departed.

A few minutes later it was Molsk who got up and left.

Algy, seeing what was about to happen from the way Molsk had pushed back his chair, was already on the way to the door.

Karkoff was evidently in no hurry. He was smoking a cigar, and not until he had finished it did he call for his bill. His departure was leisurely.

'You might as well see where he goes,' Biggles told Bertie.

Biggles, now alone, having no purpose in staying, paid his bill and made his way back to the office, satisfied that the primary purpose of the lunch had been achieved in that everyone now knew the suspects by sight. He was a little puzzled over the way the other party had broken up. He could only suppose they had different tasks to do but did not waste mental energy in a futile effort to guess what they might be. Von Stalhein had not turned up at the restaurant for lunch, as Biggles thought he might. Apparently he had decided to keep out of the way, which taking all the circumstances into account was understandable.

Algy was the first of the others to return. All he had to report was that Molsk had gone to the continental platform at Victoria Station and there met the boat train from Dunkirk. He had watched the passengers off, presumably to no purpose as he had then gone to the hotel in the Cromwell Road.

Bertie came in next. Karkoff had gone straight home. He had watched the hotel for a time but had not seen him go out again.

When Ginger came in it turned out that he had been farther afield, to London Airport, where Rallensky had checked the passengers who had come in on the regular

Berlin plane. Apparently he had seen no one of interest to him for he had then gone home.

'It seems as though we've been wasting our time,' remarked Ginger moodily, when he had heard the reports of the others.

'I wouldn't say that,' Biggles told him. 'On the contrary, I find this very interesting. We've made at least one point. It now looks as if the person these thugs are after isn't here yet; and, moreover, they don't know how or when he's coming. Why otherwise should they watch both ports of entry, sea and air. I suspect that means something else.'

'What else could it mean?' asked Ginger.

'It could well mean that enemy agents on the Continent have lost track of the man they're after. If they knew where he was they could phone Karkoff and so save him the trouble of watching both the boat trains and the air terminus. Obviously they have reason to think that the man who is to be done away with will make for England. These factors, taken together, could explain why Karkoff and his precious pals have been hanging about for a week or more. They also raise more difficult questions.'

'Aren't they difficult enough already?' questioned Bertie. 'What other questions could there be?'

Does this wretched man who is to be murdered know it? I'm beginning to take a different view from Von Stalhein. He was sure that to necessitate the employment of Karkoff, the number one killer, the victim must be someone on a high level of importance, probably a diplomat. Of course, the word important is a matter of degree. I mean, a man can be important in one respect and not in another. The fact that the Security people haven't been detailed to guard anyone suggests to me that the man we're concerned with comes into a different category from the one we first assumed. He may not even be a politician. He may not be known to us. It's my guess that he's more important to someone behind the Iron Curtain than he is to us. Who the deuce can it be?' Biggles tapped a cigarette irritably on the back of his hand.

'I don't see how we can hope to get a line on him,' said Algy. 'We know so little.'

'One thing we do know is, Karkoff is here, and according to Von Stalhein he's a cold-blooded professional murderer. I must accept that. Von Stalhein is an old hand at espionage, and he wouldn't fool about with a disguise, and go to the trouble of sending me an anonymous letter, without a thundering good reason. I wouldn't go so far as to say he's scared. We know him too well for that. But he's taking no chances. Neither would I were I in his position. As an escapee from a political prison he might be the man they're after, but he doesn't think so. He's been in this country for so long that it will be assumed he has told us everything he knows, so the only motive for killing him would be revenge. Even if that were so it's unlikely, he thinks, that Karkoff – who knows him by sight – would be sent to do a job which a lesser thug might do. We're certainly faced with a poser, and it isn't easy to see what we can do about it. Every time there's an air crash I shall wonder if we've missed the boat.'

'We might shadow the Karkoff gang trusting that eventually they'll lead us to the man due to be murdered,' offered Ginger.

'We should then know the answer too late. All we should find at the end of the trail would be a corpse.'

'It's queer Von Stalhein can't offer a suggestion,' said

Algy. 'He must keep in touch with events on the Continent.'

'When I last saw him he had no more idea than we have.'

Bertie stepped in. 'I'm not much good at this sort of thing but it seems to me that this stinker Karkoff is as much at sea as we are.'

'Except that he must know who he's looking for, which is something we don't know, and without a clue to work on are not likely to know. The Air Commodore can't have struck the scent or he'd have got in touch. Well, we might as well go home. We can do our guessing as well there as here.'

They locked up and took a taxi to the flat.

As they walked through the hall Biggles automatically glanced at the post-box and seeing a letter in it took it out, although not until they were in their quarters did he look at it. 'From Von Stalhein,' he said. 'Anyway, it's in the same handwriting as the anonymous note,' he went on, opening the envelope and removing the letter. 'No address. No signature, so he's still taking no chances. Listen to this.' He read:

' "I have been going through back numbers of newspapers for anything I may have missed. Three weeks ago there was a minor purge in East Berlin. One of the men arrested was *Oberst* Hans Roth, Underminister of Defence. Since the arrests a number of refugees have crossed from East Germany to the West. Roth may have escaped and been one of them. He would have so much information that it would be necessary to silence him. He would not dare to stay in Germany where he is known by sight to many people. He may have fled to England or be trying to reach this country. Burn this note." '

Biggles crumpled the letter, put it in an ash-tray and set fire to it. 'What are we to make of that?' he said quietly.

'He obviously thinks this fellow Roth might be the man Karkoff is after,' answered Algy.

'The question is, did he get away? We should be able to check on that. Our Intelligence people would know. If he did there might be something in what Von Stalhein says. The Air Commodore could find out.' Biggles looked at the clock. 'He may still be in his office. I don't like using the phone for this sort of thing so I'll get a cab and dash back to the Yard. It won't take long.'

He went out.

In less than an hour he was back, and the expression on his face as he walked in prepared the others for his news. 'No use,' he said.

'So he's still in prison?' queried Ginger.

'Worse. A fortnight ago he was tried for plotting against the State, sentenced to death and shot the next morning.'

'Not so good,' murmured Algy. 'I suppose there's no way of proving that? I mean, reports from that part of the world are not always correct.'

'I'd say this one is true otherwise there would have been no need for any report to be issued. Had Roth escaped, and I imagine only by a miracle could he have done that, the soft pedal would have come down on the story.'

'So we're back where we were.'

'Looks like it. I'm afraid this is where we find ourselves bogged down. I've no personal interest in Roth, anyhow. What worries me is the possibility of perfectly innocent people being killed at the same time as the man who's been put on the spot. These devils might sabotage an aircraft with a full load of passengers on board. It isn't all that difficult to slip a parcel containing a time bomb in the luggage compartment. It isn't possible to open every suitcase being loaded into every machine. The search would take longer than the flight. Von Stalhein assures me that this sort of devilment has actually been done, although the disaster was written off as an accident.'

'We might tail Karkoff and Co. and get a lead that way,' suggested Bertie.

'It isn't practicable. To keep a twenty-four hour watch on three men who might not always be together would be too big a job for us to tackle, particularly as we haven't been detailed for the assignment. The Chief hasn't actually told me to lay off the case but I don't think he's too keen on us getting involved in a matter which isn't really our cup of tea.'

'In that case why not hand it over to the Security people, or the Counter-espionage Branch, and leave them to get on with it – if you see what I mean.'

'Because that would mean telling them everything; how we got on to the business. That would mean bringing Von Stalhein into the picture and he particularly asked me to keep him out of it. Moreover, as I argued with the Chief, when a lot of people are let into a secret there's always a risk of a leakage. Anyway, it's all too vague. The Security people would want to know who they were to guard. We don't know so we can't tell them. As for Counter-espionage, we have no reason to suppose that the man booked to be murdered is an enemy agent coming here to do us a mischief. In fact, if, as it seems, he is to be silenced, his purpose might be to do us a good turn.'

Said Ginger: 'Von Stalhein obviously doesn't know

that this chap Roth has had his chips. Don't you think you should tell him?'

'Yes, I shall have to do that. It means going round to him. He isn't on the phone and he wouldn't thank me for putting anything in writing. His own position isn't entirely safe. He should be at home at this hour. I'll slip along to his quarters and join you at the French restaurant round the corner for a meal as soon as I'm through. See you presently.'

Biggles picked up his hat, went out, found a taxi and in twenty minutes was paying the driver outside the building where, on the top floor, his one-time enemy lived in a modest flat. Going up he knocked on the door which was opened by the man he had come to see, one hand in the pocket of a dressing-gown.

'It's only me. You won't need your gun,' greeted Biggles, smiling faintly.

When they were inside Von Stalhein put the automatic in a drawer of a desk. 'One never knows,' he remarked dryly.

'Sorry to worry you at this hour but I've a spot of news I thought you might care to have,' went on Biggles. 'I got your note, for which many thanks, and followed it up. Was the man you mentioned a friend of yours?'

'I wouldn't go as far as that, but when I lived in the same part of the world I knew him and his family fairly well. Why?'

'Then you may be sorry to hear he's dead. A fortnight ago he was tried for treason, sentenced to death and shot the next day.'

Von Stalhein pulled a grimace. 'I can't say I'm surprised. They never really trusted him. So they were taking no chances of him coming over to this side. He knew too much. I wonder what happened to his family.

They, too, must have known too much for the good of their health.'

'What family had he?'

'When I knew them, a wife, a son, and a daughter. Both children would now be in their late teens. I'm sorry for them. You know how it is. Unless they made a quick getaway and managed to cross the border into West Berlin it's unlikely we shall ever hear of them again.'

'What a country to live in,' breathed Biggles. 'Suppose they managed to get across into West Berlin what would they do – not that I can see any way of helping them there.'

'Naturally, they'd go into hiding. They have, or used to have, friends in West Berlin. They might stay with them, anyway for a time. Why do you ask?'

'I'm still wondering if there could be any connection between this Roth affair and Karkoff being here. I mean, could he be after Roth's wife?'

Von Stalhein thought for a moment. 'I'd hardly think so. Why should she come here?'

'She'd be safer here than in Germany. Surely she'd realise that even if she and her family got into West Berlin it wouldn't take East German agents long to track her down. It doesn't need me to tell you the country must be crawling with spies.'

'Oh, yes, they'd get her if she stayed there,' agreed Von Stalhein. 'No doubt she'd be more worried for her children, Moritz the boy, and Margareta the girl, than for herself.'

'Would she know you'd been given political asylum in this country?'

'Her husband would know. He may have told her. She knew me.'

'Would they know your address in London?'

'Most unlikely. I've done my utmost to keep it secret. That is why I receive no letters here and have no telephone.'

'So even if they got to London there could be no chance of them calling on you for help?'

'None.'

'Would you help them?'

'Certainly.'

'Could you make a guess at anyone who would give them accommodation if they got through into West Berlin?'

Again Von Stalhein searched his memory. 'I remember one particular family with whom they were extremely friendly although that was some time ago. I dined at their house several times with the Roths. Their names were Max Lowenhardt and his wife. Their daughter Anna was engaged to marry Moritz Roth so that would be a close tie.'

'Would you tell me where they lived or is that asking too much?'

'For what purpose do you want their address?'

'I must find out why Karkoff is here. There is just a possibility, as they must know too much, that it might be the Roth family, or one of them. The first thing to establish, therefore, is if they managed to escape to West Berlin. From what you tell me the Lowenhardts should know. If they don't I shall question our Security officers on the spot. Believe me, I shall be very careful.'

'Very well. When I knew the Lowenhardts they had a house on the Antonstrasse, Number seventy-one.'

'Thanks. I'll let you know how I get on. Now I'll get along. By the way, in case you don't know, Karkoff and Co. are still lunching at the Adlon. They are watching the arrivals from Germany at London Airport, also the boat trains at Victoria Station, so it looks as if they haven't found what they came for. It was queer that you and Karkoff should choose to eat at the same restaurant.'

'Not entirely. The name should tell you why. The people who run the Adlon are Germans. So are many of the customers. You know what they say – birds of a feather . . .'

'Ah. So that was how it happened. I'll be seeing you.' Biggles departed, and went direct to the little French restaurant near the flat where more often than not, when they were all at home, they had their evening meal.

'Well, and how did you get on?' asked Algy, when Biggles had joined the others at their table.

'It's a bit early to say. Von Stalhein was as helpful as he could be. Told me all about a certain family. We needn't mention names. I'll tell you about it later. In the morning I shall go to Berlin and make a few inquiries on the spot. I should get back the same day.'

'How will you go? In one of our own machines?'

'No. It isn't worth while. If I can get a seat I might as well travel on one of the regular services from London Airport and let someone else do the work – I'll deal with that when we get home. For the present, what are we eating?'

Biggles reached for the menu card.

# CHAPTER 4

# LADY IN TROUBLE

BIGGLES had only one purpose in going to Berlin, and
that was to call on the Lowenhardts to ascertain if they
knew anything about the fate of the Roth family. They
should, he thought, be able to confirm or deny the death
of Hans Roth, ex-Under-minister of Defence in East
Berlin. If in fact he had been executed there would be an
end to the matter; but if he was still alive, and free, he
might well be the man Karkoff was after. As a clue to
Karkoff's purpose in London this was so slender that
Biggles did not seriously expect success, but as it was all
he had to work on he felt bound to follow it up.

He had no reason to suppose that the trip would in-
volve him in any sort of danger, or even complications.
Difficulties, perhaps, such as getting the Lowenhardts to
talk; but nothing more. It was not as if he intended to
invite suspicion, or call attention to himself, by entering
the Eastern, Soviet dominated, sector of the city. West
Berlin, where the Lowenhardts lived, was free for visitors to come and go as they pleased. Wherefore on arrival he took no precautions to conceal his destination,
but engaging a taxi asked to be taken to the Antonstrasse, Number seventy-one. It may be that on this
occasion he underestimated the magnitude of the oppos-
ing spy system.

Having paid off his car he turned to the house, a place of medium size, one of a row standing practically on the road. That is to say, there was no front garden, merely three steps leading from the pavement to the door. He rang the bell. Almost at once he saw one of the window curtains move slightly, which told him someone was at home and that he was under observation.

After a short delay the door was opened and he found himself confronted by a remarkably pretty girl of about seventeen years of age. Her eyes were blue and a wreath of corn-coloured hair, in plaits, was coiled on her head. The way she was dressed told him she was not a house-maid.

Smiling what he hoped was a disarming smile he raised his hat, saying: *'Guten Morgen, gnadiges Fräulein.* Is Herr Lowenhardt at home?' Naturally he spoke in German.

*'Nein. Herr Lowenhardt ist nicht zu Hause,'* was the answer, given somewhat coldly.

'I am sorry,' returned Biggles. 'A friend of mine, and yours, I think, who now lives in England, asked me to deliver a message. You will remember him no doubt. Herr von Stalhein. Could it be that you are Anna?'

The question was not answered. The girl's eyes were searching Biggles' face. 'Do you mean you have come from England?' she spoke in English.

Biggles raised his eyebrows. 'So you speak English.'

'I have lived in England.'

'Good. Is your mother at home?'

'My mother is dead.'

'I beg your pardon. Then as your father is out may I talk to you? What I have to say will not take long.'

'Come in. It is better not to talk here.'

They went in. She closed the door and led the way into a sitting-room that overlooked the street. From the window she surveyed as much of the street as it was possible to see. Turning away she said: 'You say you have a message?'

'Yes.'

'What is your name please?'

'Bigglesworth. Rather a silly name, I know, but I caught it from my father. I have known Erich von Stalhein . . .'

'He lived in East Berlin.'

'That is true, but now he lives in London.'

'What is the message?'

'News has reached him that a man you both knew, Hans Roth, is dead. Is it true.'

'So it is said. What of it?'

'Von Stalhein is anxious to know if his family is safe.'

The girl's face had turned pale. 'Why should he think we would know?'

Biggles' eyes went to the ring on her finger. 'Perhaps because he knew Anna Lowenhardt was engaged to marry Moritz Roth.'

The girl was silent.

Biggles fired a direct question. 'You *are* Anna Lowenhardt?'

'That is my name, and that is all I can tell you.'

Biggles could understand the girl's reluctance to talk freely to a stranger. 'Is that the message I am to take back?'

'Why did not Herr von Stalhein come himself?'

'There are reasons, which you should know, why he would not care to be seen in Berlin. He asked me to say he is willing to do anything in his power to help the family of Herr Roth.'

'They are not here.'

'He did not think they would be but he thought you might know where they were.'

'How could he help if he will not come to Berlin.'

'He thought the Roths might come to England.'

Anna's eyes were cloudy with suspicion. 'I don't know where they are.'

'I have a feeling you have been asked that question before,' said Biggles softly.

'I have said all I have to say.'

'Even if I told you that if the Roths have gone to England they could be in great danger?'

Anna went white to the lips. 'From whom?'

'Certain East German agents with bad reputations have arrived in London.'

'How do you know?'

'I have seen them. I know their names. Von Stalhein knows them, too. He has good reason.'

Still Anna hesitated.

'You don't trust me,' prompted Biggles.

'I trust no one. Neither would you if you lived here.'

Biggles realised how the girl was feeling. Living in a city torn apart by strife and the threat of war she was a prey to doubts and fears. 'Very well,' he said quietly. 'I will not press you with any more questions but I would assure you I come as a friend, which is, I think, something you need badly at this moment. I will give you my address in London. I will not write it so you must remember it. Should the Roths go to England, if they will call at this address arrangements will be made for them to meet Herr von Stalhein.'

'You really think they would be in danger even in England?'

'Remembering the position Moritz' father held in the Eastern Sector they would be in danger anywhere. They must be numbered among the unfortunate people who know too much for the peace of mind of some we need not mention. Anyone helping them would be in danger, too.'

'I understand what you mean.' Again Anna crossed to the curtain and looked up and down the street. 'I think it is safe for you to go now.'

Biggles frowned. 'Am I to understand that this house is being watched?'

'I don't know. Perhaps. Anyone who knew Herr Roth will fall under suspicion. I have not been out to see.' Anna smiled sadly. 'You do not know how lucky you are to live in England.'

'What took you there?'

'When I left school I went to England for a year to learn the language. I worked as a governess.'

Biggles offered his hand. *'Auf wiedersehen, gnädiges Fräulein.* We may not meet again, but should you come to England and need a friend you have my address. I shall go straight back home and tell Herr von Stalhein what you say. You will tell your father of my visit when he returns home.'

*'Ja wohl.'*

She saw him out and he walked on down the street, looking for a taxi, thinking over their conversation. He suspected she could have told him more but he could appreciate the position she was in. He soon picked up a taxi and asked to be taken to the airport.

On arrival he found he had half an hour to wait for the next plane to London. He had his return ticket so he bought a newspaper, found a seat in the waiting-hall and settled down to kill time, occasionally, purely from habit, looking around at other travellers coming in and leaving by the various services.

The departure time of his own plane was drawing near when his attention was drawn to the behaviour of two men who had just arrived by car, apparently in a hurry, but were now standing close together on one side of the general flow of traffic. Both were looking in the same direction and there was something so alert, so tense, in their manner, that he knew from experience they were watching somebody. For an uncomfortable moment he thought he was the target of their interest; but then he saw they were looking past him at someone a little farther along.

Raising his paper as if to turn over the page, but actually to hide his face, he looked to see who it was. A young woman, smartly dressed, with the collar of her fur coat turned up, carrying a small suitcase, was pacing up and down either with impatience or in a state of anxiety. The next time she turned and he was able to see her face any ideas he may have had were banished in a flash. It was the girl he had just left. Anna Lowenhardt.

His first thought was, did she know she was being watched? No, he decided quickly, she did not, for she never so much as glanced in the direction of the two men who had her under observation. Clearly, he would have to do something about it, and quickly, for the number of his flight was now being called over the public address system. Getting up he walked fast enough to overtake her as she made for the passage to the airfield. Catching up with her he said tersely: 'Anna, don't look round but you are being followed.' He dropped his newspaper as an excuse to keep near her. As he picked it up he said: 'Where are you going?'

Anna faltered for a moment, as was excusable, but she did not look round. She took a quick look and saw who was speaking. 'To London', she answered.

'Keep walking. Are you going on this flight?' Biggles spoke without looking at her.

'Yes.'

'So am I. What is the number of your seat?'

'Twenty.'

'Do exactly as I tell you. I shall get as near to you as I can. Follow me.'

Biggles strode on and was one of the first to enter the aircraft. To the air hostess he said: 'If all seats are not reserved I would like to sit as near as possible to number twenty.'

The girl looked at her papers. 'There are some spare seats. You may have the one next to twenty if you like.'

'Thank you.' Biggles went on and took his place. Within a minute Anna was beside him. He stood up to allow her to have the window seat, he himself taking the one next to the gangway. 'Behave as if we're strangers,' he said quietly, without looking at her. 'We can talk presently.'

Nothing more was said. The other passengers took their places, among them the two men who were following Anna. They sat towards the rear. At the finish, when the door was closed, only about half the seats were occupied. Then, after the usual departure routine the machine was airborne, climbing as it headed westwards.

Biggles allowed a few minutes to pass. Then, speaking quietly, he said: 'Did you know you were being followed?'

'No.'

'Behave as if you still didn't know. Don't worry. You'll be safe with me.'

Anna did not answer.

Biggles stopped the steward, who was serving drinks, as he passed. 'I want to send a radiogram.'

'Very good, sir. I'll bring you a form.'

The form was brought. Biggles wrote his message, addressing it to Algy at Scotland Yard asking for a car to meet the plane at London Airport. He would see him in the Customs hall. As he handed the form back to the steward he gave him a quick glimpse of his police pass. 'I'd like that signal to be sent off as quickly as possible.'

The steward nodded understandingly. 'I'll see to it, sir.'

Anna, who had of course seen all this, now spoke. 'Who are you?' she asked curiously.

Biggles knew this question would sooner or later be asked and realised that the time had come for it to be answered. He had refrained from volunteering the information when he had called at the house seeing no reason to provide it. Moreover, he was afraid it might alarm the girl unnecessarily. But the situation was now altogether different. Holding the police pass, open, low on his knees, he said: 'If you look down at what I am holding in my hands you will see the answer to your question.' He gave her a few seconds to read it and then put the pass back in his pocket. 'Now do you understand?'

'Yes. Thank you. But why are you doing this?'

'Because you, or someone you know, may be in danger. Now listen carefully. When we land you must do as I tell you. You will have to trust me. When we arrive it will not be necessary for you to get on the official coach because a police car is meeting us. You will get in the car and go with the driver. I shall follow later. I must see where the men who are following you go. You understand?'

'Yes. So they are on the plane?'

'They are sitting behind us – don't look round. It would be better if they did not know you were aware of what they are doing.'

'Do you know these men?'

'I have never seen them before.'

'How did you know they were following me?'

'It's my business to notice such things. I knew they were watching somebody before I saw who it was. They must have seen you leave your house. You said you thought it might be watched. Now you know. You must also know *why* you are being watched.'

Anna did not answer.

Biggles went on. 'You made up your mind very suddenly to go to London, didn't you?'

'Yes.'

'Was it as a result of my visit?'

'Yes.'

'Does your father know you are on your way to England?'

'He will know when he returns home. I left a note with our housekeeper.'

'You can trust her?'

'Absolutely.'

'You are going to England to see someone – is that it?'

'I hope so.'

'Couldn't you have written a letter?'

'Letters are dangerous.'

'Quite right. But we can talk about these matters later. When we arrive I shall see that you go straight

through Customs without an examination. You have
nothing you ought to declare?'

'Nothing.'

'Your passport is in order?'

'It is the one I had when I came to London to work. I
think it is still valid.'

'Good. Then there should be no trouble.'

'Won't these men follow me when we land?'

'No doubt they hope to but I think I can prevent
that.'

'How?'

'By arranging for them to be delayed in
Customs.' Biggles smiled. 'Their examination will be
very thorough. You see, I am a special sort of police
officer well known at London Airport.'

Anna looked at him. 'You are very kind. Why do you
do all this for someone you don't know?'

'Shall we say because in helping you we may help
other people to become our friends.'

The aircraft roared on. They did not speak again, one
reason being that Biggles was anxious that the girl
should get a grip on the situation that had arisen before
pressing her with more questions, and, for another, he
wanted to think about it himself. It had come about so
suddenly that there had been no time to anticipate what
the outcome might be. He had set out that morning with
the intention of trying to get a line on Karkoff's purpose
in coming to London. Was what he was doing linked up
with that or was he right off the track?

There was still no clear indication. If he was right,
Anna, when she had gained confidence, might provide
the answer. Should he be wrong it would look as though
he had saddled himself with a responsibility he might
have cause to regret. But as things had fallen out, he

pondered, he could not have acted otherwise than he had. To play knight errant to a damsel in distress was a task he would not have gone out of his way to undertake. But there it was. The girl was obviously in greater danger than she realised and he would have to give her a helping hand.

His train of thought was brought to an end by the arrival of the aircraft over its terminus. 'You know what you have to do,' he said softly.

'Yes. I shall follow you closely with my case.'

'That's right. Don't attempt to see the men who followed you.'

Having disembarked Biggles made straight for the Customs hall, taking no more notice of Anna than a surreptitious glance to make sure she was near him. When he entered the hall the first person he saw was Algy, waiting for him just inside the entrance, his police authority having gained him admission.

Algy spoke first. 'Karkoff is here.'

'The devil he is! Where is he?'

'In the public hall.'

'Did he see you? He might have recognised you from the Adlon.'

'I don't think so. I walked straight in here. He had to wait outside.'

'You've got the car?'

'Yes.'

'Okay. I've got a girl with me.'

Algy's eyebrows went up.

'She's being tailed. I'm handing her over to you. She's beside me, in the fur coat. Anna Lowenhardt. I'll get her case marked. Take her home. I'll come later. That's all.'

Biggles turned. The Chief Customs Inspector, standing behind the examiners who lined the counter, gave him a nod of recognition. Biggles beckoned him over. 'The lady on my right in the fur coat. You might put your mark on her case. It's okay.'

'Need any help?'

'No thanks. I can manage.'

The official took a step to where Anna was standing with her case on the counter and made the necessary chalk mark on it.

Biggles spoke to her briefly, still without looking at her. 'Go with my friend here. He'll take care of you.'

Algy walked towards the public hall, Anna following.

'What goes on?' asked the Customs man.

'I haven't time to tell you now. You see the two men just coming in?'

'Yes.'

'You might hold 'em up for a few minutes to give Algy Lacey a chance to get clear.'

'Have they got anything on 'em?'

'I don't know. They're enemy agents shadowing the girl I brought in.'

The official walked along his side of the counter to where the men were waiting with an impatience they did not attempt to conceal, to be cleared.

Pulling down the brim of his hat and turning up the collar of his coat Biggles went through to the main hall. Karkoff was there, ready to watch the passengers as they emerged. His attention being on them he did not so much as glance in the direction of Biggles, who took up a position to watch.

It was a good five minutes before the two shadowers came out, walking quickly and apparently annoyed by the delay. Karkoff went straight to them. There was a short argument, or explanation, at the end of which all

three strode to the main exit. They spent a minute looking about them, presumably hoping to see Anna. One of
them looked in the coach waiting to take the air passengers to the terminal building in London. He came back
shaking his head. Upon this Karkoff called the first of a
line of waiting taxis.

Biggles took the second. 'Follow the cab in front,' he
ordered, and taking his seat sat back with a smile of
satisfaction, feeling for his cigarette case.

He was not surprised when the leading cab made its
way to Kensington and pulled up at the Cosmolite
Hotel. It was all he wanted to know.

'Okay,' he told his driver, and gave him his home
address.

CHAPTER 5

# ANNA TALKS

BIGGLES returned home to find everyone sitting round the table drinking tea, apparently on the best of terms. He pulled up a chair and joined the party.

'Everything go off all right?' asked Algy.

'Yes. Much as I expected after you'd told me Karkoff was there. He met the two off the plane and the three of them went to the hotel in the Cromwell Road. So we do at least know they are associated, and that means there's a link-up with Anna. Not necessarily with her, of course, but with her father and through him certain friends.' Biggles was watching Anna's face as he spoke, but her expression did not change. 'Does the name Karkoff mean anything to you?' he inquired of her.

She shook her head. 'Nothing. Should it?'

'I hope not,' answered Biggles vaguely. He looked back at Algy. 'Has Anna told you what happened?'

'She has given us the broad facts.'

'Then I needn't go over them again.' Biggles turned again to Anna. 'I'm afraid this may alarm you, but you must realise by now that you may be in danger. Just how serious that danger may be I don't know – yet. I want to help you, but if I am to do that you will have to help me.'

'How can I help you?'

'By answering truthfully some questions I am going to ask you.'

'I will do my best to answer.'

'Good. Do you know why those two men were following you?'

'I think so. They must have been watching the house and saw me leave.'

'Do you know who they are?'

'No.'

'Whoever they were they would be enemies?'

'No one else would watch us.'

Biggles put the leading question. 'Were they watching your house because they knew you were friendly with the Roths?'

'That is the only reason I can think of.'

'So the Roths *did* escape to West Berlin?'

'Yes.'

'And they came to you?'

'Yes.'

'Are they in your house in the Antonstrasse now?'

'No. Not now.'

'How long did they stay with you?'

'One night.'

'Why only one night?'

'We invited them to stay but they refused, saying it was not fair to us. Spies would soon know where they were and that would put us in great danger.'

'Had the Roths any money?'

'A little. Not much. My father gave them some.'

'So that they could come to England?'

Anna hesitated.

'I can understand why you would rather not say much about the Roths, but if you will be frank it would save much time and trouble. It might also be the means of saving the lives of the Roths. Enemy agents are in this country looking for them, and when they find them they will kill them. Now tell me. Did the Roths come to England?'

Anna moistened her lips. 'Yes.'

'And you know where they are?'

'I think so.'

'You're not sure?'

'I know where they were going but they may not have stayed long.'

'And you decided, after my visit to your house this morning, to come to England to see them?'

'Yes.'

'Why?'

'To warn them of their danger. I dare not write a letter because it would not be safe.'

'My information is, Herr Roth was shot. Do you know that for certain?'

'Yes.'

'Can you think of any reason why the people who did that should be so anxious to find the rest of the family?'

'I can only tell you what Moritz told me when they were in our house. His father had for some time been under suspicion of having sympathies with the West. He was making plans for them all to escape when he was arrested. But he had made provision for that. He had some important papers. He gave them to Moritz.'

'What did he hope to gain by that?'

'He thought they would be a safeguard for the family. In return for the papers the East German government would leave them in peace.'

Biggles pulled a grimace. 'That was a dangerous game to play.'

'I can see that now.'

'What happened?'

'The secret police came to the house where Frau Roth lived and searched it for the papers.'

'So they knew the papers existed?'

'They must have done.'

'Did they find them?'

'No. Moritz had hidden them too well. But he knew the police would come again, and if the papers could not be found they would all be arrested, and perhaps tortured to make them speak. They did not wait for that. During the night, Frau Roth, with Moritz and Margareta, by means of a rope, escaped from a back bedroom window. They knew where to go. Plans had been made for that. Before daylight they were in West Berlin. This, you must understand, was before the concrete walls were built.'

'Has Moritz still got those papers?'

'He had when they left us.'

Biggles looked shocked. 'My God! That's like walking about with a bottle of nitro-glycerine in his pocket.' He looked at the others. 'Now I'm beginning to see daylight.' He turned back to Anna. 'What does Moritz intend to do with these deadly documents?'

'I think he still has an idea of using them as a weapon against the men who killed his father. It gives him a hold over them.'

'I'd say more likely to give them a hold over him. I don't know how important these papers are, but I can only imagine they must be vital for the enemy to send here a gang of men known to be murderers.' Looking at Anna very seriously Biggles went on: 'You had better know that one of them was at the airport to meet the two men who were following you.'

'But why should they follow *me*?' cried Anna.

'In my considered opinion because they hoped you would lead them to where the Roths are living. Had I not been there to prevent it you would have done that, I believe.'

'Yes. I would have gone straight to the Roths.' Anna's face was ashen, presumably at the thought of what might have happened.

'Then I take it they are in London.'

'Hampstead. They went there with a letter of introduction from me. I know the people. That is where I worked when I was here. The man of the house is a dentist and a German, now naturalised. He came here before the war. He is a Jewish gentleman so he knows what it means to be persecuted. He has a large house and it was the only place I could think of. Was it true what you told me about Herr von Stalhein?'

'Of course. How, otherwise, would I have known of you, and your address? Would you like me to let him know you are here?'

'That is as you wish. Is there any reason?'

'He might be helpful. Do you still want to see the Roths, even though it might be dangerous for you, and for them?'

'But yes. That is why I came here.'

'What clothes have you brought with you?'

'Only a spare blouse besides the coat and skirt I am wearing now. There was no time to pack. I did not think I would need more, because as soon as I had seen Frau Roth, to tell her what you had told me, I would have gone straight back home.'

'Where was your father when I called?'

'He had gone to the college.'

'What college?'

He is Professor of European History at the university.'

'I didn't know that. I don't think Von Stalhein could have known it or he would have told me.'

'He was only recently promoted.'

'Ah! That probably explains it. I imagine your father speaks English?'

'For his work he must speak and read several languages, including English.'

'Do you think there is any chance of him, when he reads your note, of following you to England?'

'I don't know. He might. Why?'

'Does he know where the Roths are living here?'

'Yes. This was arranged between us.'

Biggles bit his lip. 'Pity. It means that if he did come here that is where he would go, expecting to find you there.'

'Without a doubt. He would not know where else to look for me.'

'Then we shall have to find a way to prevent that from happening. It would be a tragedy if he did what you would have done had I not stopped you.'

'Now that the men who were watching the house have followed me here there may be no one to keep watch in the Antonstrasse,' said Anna, hopefully.

'I wouldn't care to reckon on that. I'd say the men who followed you have already been in touch with their employers to report what happened, and how they came to lose you.'

'But my father! If the secret police know the Roths stayed in our house they may kill him.' Anna was visibly upset.

'I think they would be more likely to watch him, so that needn't worry us unless he came rushing over here to find you and see the Roths. But it's getting late. The first thing is to see you safely in an hotel for the night. Stay indoors until you hear from me. The men who followed you from Berlin know you by sight and no doubt they'll be busy looking for you. Tomorrow we will talk again. Meanwhile, you will have to decide if it would be wise for you, after what has happened, to go to the house where the Roths are staying. I may be able to advise you when I know exactly where that is. If necessary a meeting could be arranged somewhere else.'

'After I have seen them shall I go back to Berlin?'

'It's too early to say. Much now depends on what your father does. Leave it to me. That's enough for now. Try not to worry too much. I will take you to an hotel where your enemies will not be likely to find you. Tomorrow we will talk again. One last thing. A strange request, you may think. Will you lend me that brooch you're wearing?'

Anna stared. 'Of course,' she agreed, unfastening the ornament, a simple gold pin with three small pearls in a row. 'Please take care of it. It was a present from my father.' She put it on the table.

'Thank you,' acknowledged Biggles, leaving the jewel where she had laid it. 'You might phone for a cab, Ginger.'

Ginger complied.

'Where are you going to take Anna?' asked Bertie, while they waited.

'The Barchester would be as good as anywhere. It's quiet and it's handy. Stick around. I shan't be many minutes and I shall want to talk to you when I get back.'

The door bell rang. 'There's your cab,' said Ginger.

'Come along, Anna,' said Biggles. 'I'll take your case.'

'You are being very kind.'

'It's always a pleasure to help a lady,' returned Biggles gallantly, as they went out.

In twenty minutes he was back. 'That's fixed that,' he said. 'She should be all right there. If Karkoff and Co. try ringing every hotel in London to ask if she's there it should take them a long time to get round to the Barchester.'

'Did you book her in under her own name?' Algy asked the question.

'Yes. I thought it better. On a business of this sort one never knows what's going to crop up and there could be all sorts of complications if the name in the register didn't tally with the one on her passport.' Biggles sat down. 'It begins to look as if I didn't waste my time going to Berlin. We're running on a hot scent. Bar a series of coincidences the Roths are the people Karkoff is after. If those papers Anna mentioned are so important to the top men on the other side of the Concrete Curtain you can bet they'd be just as important to us. If Moritz is going about with them in his pocket he must be out of his mind. That's asking to be knocked on the head.'

'Why didn't you ask Anna where the Roths were staying while you were at it?' asked Bertie.

'I didn't want to press her too hard. She's still a bit nervous and we can hardly blame her for that. We'll get round to that tomorrow, when she's had time to think it over. It's her father I'm worried about now. If he comes rushing over here he's liable to drop the spanner in the gears.'

'How can we stop him?' asked Ginger.

'That'll be your job tomorrow.'

'How?' Ginger looked astonished. 'We don't know which way he'll travel.'

'I hope you'll be in time to stop him travelling at all. You're catching the next plane to Berlin. Book yourself a seat. Claim priority if necessary.'

'And what do I do when I get there?'

'It's no use messing about at this stage. Go straight to the Antonstrasse and ask to see Professor Lowenhardt. If he isn't there, wait for him. All you have to do is tell him what has happened. Say Anna is safe and under police protection. The best thing he can do is stay at home. If he should insist on coming to England he must on no account go near the Roths. If he does it may mean the death of them. If he likes he can come here. You should have no trouble in West Berlin. If it was the East side of the line it would be a different matter.'

'I'd have thought it would have been better for you to go yourself.'

'I can't be in three places at once. The first thing I must do is speak to the Air Commodore about this. He may not approve of our bashing on with work that isn't really up our alley – anyhow, not without letting him know how things stand. I must also have another chat with Anna. There's another reason why I'd rather keep out of the way. The men who followed Anna will have put two and two together. They know me by sight. They will remember me as the man who sat next to Anna in the plane and stood by her in the Customs hall. They'd be fools if they didn't realise I had a finger in the pie – particularly if Karkoff recalled he had twice seen me in the Adlon Restaurant.'

'I can see one big snag in my going to Berlin,' said Ginger doubtfully.

'What is it?'

'Will Lowenhardt see me? If he does, will he listen to me? He'll be in no state to talk to a complete stranger.

I'd expect him to be more than somewhat suspicious of everyone.'

Biggles picked up Anna's brooch, still lying on the table. 'Why do you think I asked Anna to lend me this? He'll know it's hers. He gave it to her, which is all to the good. He will at least know you must have been with her. That should smooth things out.'

'Okay. Why you wanted that brooch got us all guessing.'

'Now you know. I thought it better not to tell Anna. She's anxious enough already. What I do after I've seen her will depend on what she tells me. If she lets me know where the Roths are living I may go to see them. I might also tell Von Stalhein how things stand. After all, he put us on to this. Being a German he may be useful, in that, knowing how German minds work, he might be able to guess what the enemy will do next.'

'You won't do anything about Karkoff?' queried Algy.

'There's nothing we *can* do while he and his gang behave themselves. We must give them credit for having enough sense to keep on the right side of the law until the time comes for them to do the dirty work for which they were sent here. Now we'll have something to eat and get some sleep while we can. We may be losing some presently. Don't forget to get yourself a seat on the Berlin service, Ginger.'

'I'll do it right away.'

# CHAPTER 6

# DISAPPOINTING NEWS

THE next morning when Biggles appeared for breakfast Ginger had already departed on his mission to Berlin. However, the others were there, and as he joined them at the table he said: 'We look like having a busy day so let's get organised. For a start I shall have to see the Chief. Algy, you'd better come with me to deal with anything that may have turned up at the office. I don't know what time the Air Commodore will come in but I don't suppose it will be before half-past nine. I may be some while with him so what I suggest is this. You get the mail and anything else sorted in the office; if I'm not back with you by ten o'clock take the car, pick up Anna at the hotel and bring her round to the flat. It'll be easier to talk here. We can't very well go up to her bedroom, and it would be as well, I think, to keep out of the public lounge. So bring her to the flat and wait here till I come. That is, assuming I'm held up with the Chief.'

'I'll do that,' assented Algy.

Biggles continued. 'Bertie, what I want you to do is make an early call on Von Stalhein. I've thought a lot about this and I've decided to let him know Anna is here. You'd better tell him the circumstances in which she arrived. It might be a good thing if he came round here to meet her. If he'd rather not, say I'd be very much obliged if he'd let me know whether or not Karkoff is still having his lunch at the Adlon and how many men he has with him. The party may have increased to five. I'm wondering if the two men who followed Anna have stayed on here. They may have gone back to Berlin. Of course, it may be that Von Stalhein is now giving the Adlon a wide berth. If so you might check up yourself. If we know Karkoff's movements they might give us a line on what he intends to do next. You can use taxis or your own car, whichever you like. I think that's about all we can do until Ginger reports back from Berlin.'

'I've been doing some thinking, too,' said Algy. 'I can't see how all this is going to end. We can't go on playing watch-dog to the Roths and the Lowenhardts indefinitely.'

'Of course not. What we do will depend on the people themselves. It isn't for us to give them orders. Once the Roths have been warned that we have reason to suppose that Karkoff and his thugs are after their blood it'll be up to them to make their own arrangements. We can't do more.'

'And we can't do less,' asserted Bertie. 'This hounding decent people, like Goldilocks, from one country to another, makes my back hairs bristle.'

Biggles looked up. 'Goldilocks! Who are you talking about?'

'Anna, of course.'

'Don't get the idea this is a fairy tale.'

'You must admit she's a honey.'

Biggles frowned. 'She may be, but the thing for you to remember is, where there is honey there are bees. Watch out for 'em or you're liable to get stung.'

Bertie smiled sheepishly. 'Sorry, old boy. Only my fun.'

'All right, but let's not have too much of the Prince Charming stuff. I'm hoping Anna will tell me where the Roths are, in which case I shall probably go to see them. Her chief interest, I imagine, is in Moritz, to whom she's engaged. If I see him I'll tell him to get rid of those papers which according to Anna he has with him.'

'I can't see how any of them will be able to go back to Berlin.'

'That'll be up to them when they know the facts. They're not the only people in the miserable predicament of not being able to go home for fear of being bumped off. No matter where they go they can never feel entirely safe. Their enemies will never stop looking for them, and with their network of spies they sooner or later catch up with them. You may remember Trotsky. He went into hiding in Mexico, but they found him and knocked his brains out with an axe. Those are the sort of people we are dealing with. But let's get on with it. You both know what you have to do.'

Taking Algy with him Biggles went to the office. The Air Commodore had not yet arrived, so while he was waiting Biggles helped Algy with the mail. There was nothing that demanded urgent action. A little after nine-thirty they were informed that the Air Commodore was in his office so Biggles went along.

He was soon back, to find Algy still there.

'Well, how did he take it?' inquired Algy.

Biggles shrugged. 'So-so. He's not too happy about it. A bit peeved with me for getting involved in the first place. A lot of talk about exceeding our duties, and so on. Said we had plenty to do without going out of our way to look for trouble. Knowing how he hates to be mixed up with anything political I expected that. However, he agreed that having gone so far we'd better carry on. We couldn't just stand by and see the Roths murdered. He also saw that to start a general alarm would do more harm than good, in that Karkoff would get wind of it and set his clock accordingly. What does interest him are the papers Moritz has brought with him.'

'Naturally. If he could get his hands on those it would be a feather in his cap.'

Biggles looked at the clock. 'It's nearly ten o'clock so we might as well press on and collect Anna.'

Taking their car from the garage Biggles drove to the hotel. He went in, presently to come out with Anna. They went on to the flat. Bertie was not there, of course, having gone to see Von Stalhein.

'Now, Anna,' began Biggles, when they had made themselves comfortable. 'Did you have a good night's rest?'

'Not very. I was too worried.'

'You had some breakfast?'

'Yes, thank you.'

'Cigarette?'

'No thanks. I smoke very little.'

'All right. Now let us see if we can untangle this unhappy state of affairs. The first and most important thing is to let the Roths know there is reason to think their enemies are in England looking for them. There are two ways that can be done. You can go to them yourself, although I think that would be taking an unnecessary risk. The less you are seen outside the better. In this murky game eyes are everywhere. The alternative would be for you to tell me where they are. I would go to see them and explain the position, or bring Moritz here when you could tell him yourself. It's for you to decide. Which shall it be? Will you go out alone or tell

me where they are? You are of course at liberty to go
anywhere or do anything you wish. I am simply trying
to help you; or, if you like to put it the other way round,
to defeat the object of these villains who have come to
this country.'

'I will take your advice,' said Anna without hesi-
tation. 'I think it better that you should go to the Roths.
I did much thinking during the night and had already
made up my mind to tell you where I sent them. They
are staying with Doctor Bruno Jacobs, who lives at a
house named Westwinds, Number eleven, Bishop's
Way, Hampstead.'

'Thank you, Anna. Tell me about the Doctor.'

'He is a Jewish gentleman who was at school with my
father. He came to England many years ago. When it
was decided that I should learn to speak English my
father wrote to him and it was arranged that I should go
to him for a year as governess to the children of a rela-
tive who was then living with him, her husband having
died.'

'How long ago was this? I mean, since you returned to
Germany.'

'Nearly two years.'

'Did you keep in touch with him?'

'At first I wrote often, but not so much lately.'

'Did you write to him to say the Roths were
coming?'

'There was no time for that, things happened so
quickly. I gave Moritz a letter of introduction.'

'Did you hear from Moritz after he had arrived?'

'No. My father said not to write. It would be dangerous.'

'Was Doctor Jacobs married?'

'Yes.'

'Any children?'

'No.'

'How old would he be?'

'I never asked him that but now I think he would be more than sixty years.'

'You said he was a dentist.'

'What they call a dental surgeon.'

'Did people come to his house for treatment?'

'When I was there, all the time. He was always busy. But the last time we heard from him he said he thought he would retire. He was getting too old. But to save time could I not telephone to him, now, from here?'

'Do you know his number?'

'I have forgotten but you could find it in the telephone book.'

Biggles considered the suggestion. 'No,' he said. 'We won't do that. He would be suspicious of any stranger.'

'He might remember my voice.'

'Perhaps not. Voices can be imitated. It would be better for me to go round. It won't take long. If he wished he could telephone you here. As for me, I have papers in my pocket that would confirm my identity.' Biggles got up. 'Algy, I'll leave you to entertain Anna while I'm away. You might get her some coffee and biscuits.'

'It will be a pleasure.'

Biggles went out to the car and was quickly on his way to Hampstead. He reckoned to be there in under half an hour, and he was. He had a little difficulty in finding the street but a policeman put him right. Having located the house he locked the car and walked briskly through a small garden to the front door. In view of Doctor Jacobs' profession he expected to see the usual brass plate on the door, but was not concerned when he failed to find one. He knocked.

The door was opened by a well-dressed, middle-aged woman, clad as if for going out. She looked at the caller inquiringly.

'I would like to speak to Doctor Jacobs, please, if it is at all possible,' said Biggles politely.

'Who?'

'Doctor Jacobs.'

'I have never heard of him.'

Biggles had anticipated various receptions: but not this one. He looked at the woman's face wondering if she were lying, and decided quickly she was not. 'Then Doctor Jacobs doesn't live here?' he questioned, to gain time to recover his composure.

'He certainly does not. This is my house and my name is Smith.'

'But surely Doctor Jacobs, a dentist, used to live here?'

'He may have done for all I know. The house was unoccupied, and had been for some time, I believe, when I bought it.'

'May I ask how long ago that was?'

'About three months. If you want any information about previous tenants you'd better see the estate agents, Carson and Co., round the corner in the High Street. They handled the sale of the property. What is all this, suddenly, about people named Jacobs? I've had other people here, in the last few days, asking for them.'

'A woman with two grown-up children?'

'That's what the party looked like.'

Biggles paused while this significant remark sank home. 'I'm sorry to trouble you, but I'm a police officer,' he went on. 'I'm trying to trace the Jacobs. Do you know where the party of three went when they left here?'

'I have no idea. I gave these people the same advice as I have given you, to see Mr Carson, the estate agent. If that's all . . .'

'Yes, that's all. I'm much obliged to you.'

'Good morning.' The door was closed.

Biggles, slightly dazed by this unexpected turn in events, returned to his car with two thoughts about others in his mind. The Jacobs had gone. The Roths had apparently called at the house and had been given the same disconcerting news. Where had they gone?

He went to the High Street, found the estate agent, and after a short wait was shown into the office of Mr Carson. Producing his police pass he began: 'I'm making inquiries about a Doctor Jacobs, a dentist who until fairly recently lived at a house called Westwinds in Bishop's Way. I've been there, but a lady informs me she now owns the house.'

'That's right. A widow named Mrs Smith.'

'Can you help me to find the Jacobs?'

'I'm afraid not. In fact I know very little about Doctor Jacobs. He walked in here one day, said he had decided to sell the house and put the matter in my hands.'

'How long ago was this?'

'Must be six months. I can give you the exact date if you care to wait while I look up my file.'

'That isn't important. Did he give a reason for wanting to sell the house?'

'I remember him saying something about his wife having died, and he himself being in poor health, he found the business of trying to keep the house going, without staff, too much for him. The house remained empty for some time. It was nearly three months before I found a buyer.'

'Why did it take so long?'

'It was a difficult sale because for some reason he didn't want me to advertise in the public Press. Again, I had to sell the house complete with a lot of old-fashioned Victorian furniture. I suggested an auction sale to dispose of it, but that again, he said, would mean advertising. He gave me the impression that he was anxious to get out of the house as quickly as possible.'

'I imagine he left you a forwarding address?'

'No, oddly enough, he didn't. I think he must have found temporary accommodation somewhere near because from time to time he would look in to see if the house had been sold. He left the keys with me. Once in a while one of my assistants would show a prospective buyer over the house, and on such occasions he brought back any mail lying on the mat. The Doctor collected it here. There was not very much. I recall one or two with German postage stamps. Once he had received his cheque I think he must have left the district because I never saw him again.'

'Do you happen to know the name of his bank?'

'No. He never told me that; but then, there was no reason why he should.'

'Have you had other people here making inquiries about him?'

'Yes. There were three people together whom I took to be Germans.'

'What did you tell them?'

'Nothing. In our business we do not discuss the affairs of our clients. With you, a police officer, it is different.'

Biggles got up. 'Thank you, Mr Carson. Sorry to have taken up so much of your time. Here's my card. If by any chance you should see or hear anything of Doctor Jacobs I'd be grateful if you'd phone me at Scotland Yard. If you can't get me there you might get me at home. I'll put the number on the card.'

'I'll certainly do that.'

Biggles went out, and in anything but a cheerful mood returned to the flat. Algy and Anna were there, waiting.

'I'm afraid, Anna, I have disappointing news for you,' he said.

'Bad news?'

'It might be worse, but I couldn't call it good.'

Anna's expression changed abruptly. 'What has happened? Please tell me.'

'Doctor Jacobs no longer lives at the house in Bishop's Way. He sold it some months ago and went away without leaving an address.' Biggles went on to relate in detail the result of his inquiries.

By the time he had finished Anna was looking distressed. 'So we don't know where any of my friends are,' she said heavily.

'That, I'm afraid, is the long and short of it.'

'Couldn't the police find the Doctor?'

'They might, but it would take time. Even if we did find him it wouldn't help us to find the Roths. He can't know they are here, or that they have been to Bishop's Way. He left the house six months ago, before all this trouble started. I get the impression, from the way the Doctor acted, he didn't want to be found. Otherwise, why didn't he leave a forwarding address? That's the usual practice.'

'Could he have left it at the post office?' suggested Algy.

'Obviously not. The postman continued to leave letters at the house.'

'Why, oh why, didn't he let us know where he was going?' lamented Anna, almost tearfully.

'It looks to me as if he had reasons for not wanting anyone to know where he was going. I've no doubt it's true that he lost his wife, and that his health was worrying him, but even so, a man of his age doesn't suddenly abandon his home without good cause.'

'What you think is, something happened, perhaps in Germany, to make him afraid, so he tried to hide,' said Anna, shrewdly.

'I may be wrong, but that's how it looks to me,' admitted Biggles. 'It may have been something to do with the past. Anyway, there's nothing remarkable about a man fading into obscurity when he retires, particularly if he has no reason to tell anyone where he is going.'

Anna shook her head. 'This is terrible. It is something I could not have imagined, although, now I look back, I recall the Doctor sometimes seemed worried when he received letters from Germany. Poor Frau Roth. What would she do when she arrived at the house and found the Doctor was no longer there?'

Biggles shrugged helplessly. 'Your guess is as good as mine. Do you know if she had any other friends in England to whom she could turn for help?'

'I know of none.'

'Then money would be a problem. You say they hadn't very much.'

'Perhaps enough to live in a small hotel for a few weeks.' Anna buried her face in her hands. 'I am so bewildered that I don't know what to do.'

'For the moment, there's nothing you can do except keep out of sight as far as that is possible. If the men who followed you from Berlin were to see you it wouldn't make the problem any easier to solve.'

'Then you don't think I should go back to let my father know what has happened?'

'It would be better if you stayed here until we receive news from Germany.'

'What news? How can we receive news?'

'I see I shall have to tell you that Ginger has already left for the Antonstrasse to let your father know where you are, and that you are in safe hands. I'm sure he would be worried when he learned you had come to England. As things have turned out it's a good thing I did that, or he may have followed you and gone to Hampstead only to discover that Doctor Jacobs, the Roths, and you, had all disappeared. That would have resulted in a pretty kettle of fish, as we say. After Ginger has seen him he will at least know where you are. Should he decide to come over, so well and good. We could discuss the situation together. Now it's time we went out and had some lunch.'

# CHAPTER 7

# CITY OF FEAR

---

GINGER was in a confident mood when he arrived in Berlin, and taking a taxi, intent on getting his business finished as quickly as possible, ordered the driver to take him to his objective, the Lowenhardts' house in the Antonstrasse. As far as he was aware he was not known to anyone in the city so there seemed no point in taking precautions against being followed; but he did from time to time glance back through the rear window to check on any vehicle close behind. He saw nothing to cause him disquiet, but he did not forget he was in a city that boasted it had more spies to the square mile than any other in the world.

The Antonstrasse, as Biggles had told him, was in a residential district off the main road; and so he found it, wearing the air of quiet dignity associated with buildings of the previous century. The houses occupied one side of the street only, the other being girt by iron railings beyond which a double row of trees made a barrier between the street he was in and a busy thoroughfare.

As the taxi drew up outside Number seventy-one he noticed, and took a second look at, a car, a large black saloon, parked a little farther along in the shade of the trees. A man wearing a chauffeur's cap lounged behind the wheel reading a newspaper, apparently waiting for his employer.

Paying no further attention to it Ginger, thinking he might be some time, discharged his cab, assuming he would have no difficulty in getting another on the main road at the conclusion of his visit. This done he went up the steps to the door and rang the bell.

After a short delay it was opened by an elderly, nervous-looking woman, who from the way she was dressed was apparently a servant whom he had interrupted in some household task.

'*Was wollen sie?*' (What do you want?) she asked suspiciously.

Ginger put on his brightest smile and answered: '*Ist Professor Lowenhardt zu Hause?*' (Is Professor Lowenhardt at home?).

'*Nein*,' returned the woman curtly, and stepped back as if to close the door.

This put Ginger in a quandary. The situation, he perceived, presented a difficulty for which he was not prepared. The trouble was, he spoke only a little German, enough to get about but not enough to engage in an argument; and the woman, as he quickly confirmed, spoke no English. It had been supposed, of course, that as the Professor spoke English a knowledge of German would not be necessary. Ginger suspected that once the woman had closed the door in his face it would be hard to induce her to open it again.

He could think of only one thing to do. He had Anna's brooch ready. He took it from his pocket and held it forward.

The woman's eyes opened wide. The colour, what little there was, drained from her face. After a swift but furtive glance up and down the street, by an almost imperceptible inclination of her head she invited Ginger to enter. He did so. She closed the door behind him.

To relate in detail the laborious conversation that followed would be tedious and take up a great deal of space. The first point Ginger had to make was that Anna was in England, safe, with friends. He, an English police officer, had come from London to let Professor Lowenhardt know that in case he was worried.

When she had grasped this the woman took Ginger into a sitting-room where, lying conspicuously on a table, was a letter addressed to the Professor. It bore an English postage stamp and had not been opened, from which Ginger could only conclude, to his disappointment, that the woman had told the truth and the Professor was really not at home. He began to fear he had made a fruitless journey.

The conversation, if such it could be called, continued with the help of actions and gestures. Ginger gathered the Professor was unlikely to return home so it was no use waiting for him. He had gone away. It was some time before the woman would admit that she knew where he had gone, and Ginger got another jolt when she finally stated he had gone to London. Why? To look for Anna. When? That very morning, on the first plane. He had said nothing about coming back.

Although he had not expected this Ginger realised there was no reason to be surprised. The Professor, when he had received Anna's message, had behaved as would most fathers in the same circumstances. He had given the woman no address where he might be found, probably because he himself did not know.

Ginger decided the only thing he could do was let Biggles know what had happened as quickly as possible. He looked at his watch and saw it was past noon. The

Berlin plane would already have landed at London Airport, or would have landed before Biggles could get there. But perhaps that didn't matter. Biggles would, he thought, have learned from Anna where the Roths were staying and catch the Professor there. What he did not know, of course, was that Biggles had been to the house to discover that it had changed hands and the Roths were not there.

There was one thing that worried him. He kept looking at the letter, addressed to the Professor, on the table. It had not come from Anna, that was certain. The handwriting was that of a man, anyway. What news did the letter hold? It might be vital, yet inevitably it would now be some time before the Professor could receive it, unless . . . If the woman would let him have it he could take it home with him and perhaps deliver it the same day – if not to the Professor, to Anna.

'How long has that letter been here?' he asked.

He learned that it had only just arrived, a few minutes before he himself had called.

Ginger, like most people, was reluctant to touch someone else's mail, but here the circumstances were exceptional and he resolved to take the letter if the woman would let him have it. There could, of course, be no question of taking it by force or intimidation.

It took some time, and all his powers of persuasion, to get her to agree. Indeed, he felt she was right in refusing and he was embarrassed by having to ask. It was only the urgency, and the danger in which Anna and her friends stood, that prompted him to persist. Without Anna's brooch it is unlikely that he would have succeeded, but at the finish, on his promise to deliver the letter to Anna, if not the Professor, the same evening, he had his way. He put the envelope in his breast pocket.

That was all. There was nothing more he could do in Berlin, so he left the house, and working out how he would word a signal to Biggles walked towards the end of the street where a turn would take him to the main road and, he hoped, a taxi. Actually, he was in some doubt as to whether it was worth while sending a cable or radiogram, because if he was lucky enough to get a seat on a plane leaving shortly he might be home before the message was delivered.

As he turned the corner at the end of the street he instinctively, or from force of habit, glanced behind him, and experienced a twinge of uneasiness when he saw that the parked car, which was still in the same place when he had left the house, was now moving, cruising slowly in the same direction he had taken.

This made him think. Could it be that the driver had been watching the Lowenhardts' residence? He remembered seeing it carried an aerial – not that there was anything remarkable in that. But, naturally, he was in a state to be suspicious of anything and everything, and did not relish the thought that the man in the car might already be in touch with other enemy agents.

These vague suspicions were soon to become intensified. On reaching the main road he looked up and down for a taxi, but none was in sight. The car that had been in the Antonstrasse rounded the corner, and coming on slowly pulled up at the kerb where he stood waiting. The chauffeur, a middle-aged man, with a genial smile got out and asked if he could be of assistance. He spoke in German.

Ginger's answer was that he did not speak German.

The man repeated his question in perfect English, although with an accent.

'What gave you the idea I was English?' challenged Ginger.

'One can tell an Englishman anywhere.'

'In that case why did you speak to me in German when you speak English so well?' returned Ginger coolly. Without waiting for an answer he went on, with a note of finality in his voice to end the argument: 'Thank you, but I don't need help.'

But the man was not to be put off. 'Having nothing to do I thought I might give you a lift somewhere. Where are you going? I may be going the same way.'

'I wouldn't think of troubling you,' parried Ginger coldly, his eyes still alert for a taxi. Still none was in sight, but he was now braced for trouble, and thought it might be coming in the shape of two men striding purposefully along the pavement towards him, or the car. He did not wait to see, but turning walked away.

He was sure he would be followed, but he did not look back for a minute or two; when he did so it was to see if there was a taxi coming from that direction. The two men he had noticed were getting into the car. So that was it, he thought grimly. There was no longer any doubt about it. The Lowenhardts' house was under surveillance, and he, having been to it, was a marked man. Which all went to show how desperate the Roths' enemies were to track them down.

He walked on, his brain racing, uncomfortably sure that when he reached the airport his trackers would be behind him. If he took a taxi no doubt the driver would be questioned after he had dismissed it. He decided, for the time being, to stay where there were people about.

A few minutes later, still wondering what to do for the best – for he was anxious to get to the airport with all possible speed – he saw an opportunity and snatched at it. Again looking round he saw a British Army jeep overtaking him. An NCO was at the wheel with an officer, a lieutenant, beside him. He had seen other British service vehicles, as was to be expected since he was in the British Zone, but then they had meant nothing to him.

He stepped into the road, held up a hand, and when the jeep came to a skidding stop he spoke swiftly, at the same time holding out his police card for the officer to see. 'I'm on a spot. I've got to get back to London with an important document but I'm being shadowed by enemy agents, three of them, in a black saloon car. It's just behind you.'

'That's right, sir,' confirmed the sergeant, looking at his reflector.

'Where do you want to go?' asked the officer.

'To the airport. I haven't been able to get a taxi. If I get one now it will be followed – and there could be an accident.'

'Get in,' said the lieutenant, laconically.

Ginger got in, and the jeep shot forward at a rate which nearly threw him on the floor.

Nothing more was said. The driver seemed to enjoy the drive that followed. He did not go to the airport, as Ginger had hoped he would, but after twisting and turning at high speed through several side streets pulled up outside a military post, clearly marked as such. The lieutenant said 'Wait', and jumping down went inside. He was soon out again but did not get in the jeep. Instead, he simply said to the sergeant: 'Take this gentleman to the airport,' and would have left it at that had not Ginger called him back.

'Just a minute,' said Ginger. 'Could you send a signal for me in case I don't get an opportunity?'

'Where to?'

'Scotland Yard.'

'Write it and I'll see what I can do. As it's more or less official I might be able to get it through.'

'Thanks. A lot may hang on it.'

Taking out his notebook and addressing the message to Biggles at Scotland Yard he wrote: *Returning next plane. Our man left for England this morning. Important you meet me London Airport.* He tore out the page and handed it to the lieutenant who, with a wave, said 'Right. Good luck.'

That was all. While waiting, Ginger had kept an eye open for the black saloon, but he saw nothing of it. Riding in a service vehicle he did not expect any trouble on the drive to the airport, but what would happen when he got there was a matter for conjecture.

Arrived at the aerodrome he thanked the driver warmly, gave him a good tip 'to have a drink on the house' and hurried on to see about a seat, watching all the time for possible followers. His luck held. A BEA Viscount was due to leave in ten minutes and he was able to get a place on it. He still kept watch, and as soon as his flight number was called he went along to take his seat. It turned out to be near the tail, which suited him, because it enabled him to see the other passengers as they passed down the central gangway to places in front of him.

He saw no one he recognised, but at the last moment a man got in to take the seat next to him on the other side of the gangway. After a sidelong glance, as was natural, Ginger paid no further attention to him. He was a stranger so he could only hope he was a normal passenger. He had never been close enough to the men who had followed him near the Antonstrasse for identification.

His clothes had a German cut about them but there was nothing unusual in that. Air travel is cosmopolitan. The newspaper he took from his pocket was German.

The aircraft took off, so that settled all questions and doubts until it landed at its destination. To Ginger's relief the man in the near-by seat made no attempt to get into conversation with him; at all events, until they had crossed the English coast, when, with a friendly smile, he remarked: 'A pleasant voyage, yes?'

'Very comfortable,' agreed Ginger, a trifle curtly, to discourage further comment.

In this he was not successful, for the man went on: 'Have you made arrangements for transport when we land? I could give you a lift . . .'

'Thanks, but I have a car meeting me,' broke in Ginger, feeling he was being rude, for the offer sounded innocent enough and could have been genuine. His suspicions might be groundless but he was taking no chances. He only hoped that Biggles had received his message and was at the airport to meet him. That would iron out any trouble or interference with him should it arise.

He was not thinking so much of his personal safety as the letter he carried in his pocket. It seemed impossible that the Roths' enemies could know anything about that. But was it impossible? He thought it over. The woman had said the letter had only just arrived. The house was being watched. The events following his departure left that in no doubt. The man sitting in the car must have seen the postman call at the house so he would know a letter had been delivered. Would someone, after he had gone, have the audacity to go to the house with the object of securing it? If that had happened what would the woman say? What *could* she say?

If the postman had been seen to call it would be futile to say there was no letter. If, under threats, she admitted that a letter addressed to Professor Lowenhardt had been handed in, but was no longer there, it could only mean that he, Ginger, had taken it with him. As far as he knew he was the only person who had been to the house. Looked at like that it seemed there was a chance the enemy knew he had the letter on him. Was that what they were after? They were certainly after something, and it could hardly be him, personally, for how could they know who and what he was?

So ran Ginger's thoughts as, in twilight, with the lights coming on over the country, the air liner made its approach to the landing. He wished he had put the letter on some part of his person more difficult to get at than a pocket; but it was no use thinking about that now. With a man who might be an enemy agent sitting so close he dare not move it.

The aircraft touched down and ran to a stop. He got out as quickly as possible and, overtaking some of the passengers who were before him, walked briskly to the Customs hall. He felt, rather than saw, someone walking close behind him, and without looking was sure it was his travelling companion.

He hoped to see Biggles waiting in Customs, but a glance was enough to show he was not there. Being known to the Customs officers he was quickly passed through, and again he hurried on to the public hall having decided that if Biggles was not there he would make a run for a taxi. A glance over his shoulder revealed his travelling companion not far behind and walking at a pace calculated to overtake him. That finally settled any doubts about his purpose. Normal passengers did not walk like that.

His nerves received a jolt when he saw, standing directly in front of him, Karkoff's two assistants, Rallensky and Molsk. Was this pure chance? Were they there as part of a regular routine or had they been warned from Berlin to meet the plane? Had the man behind him made a signal to them? He didn't know, but the way all three closed on him was significant. In another moment he was pushing them aside to prevent himself from being jostled.

'What's going on,' said a voice sharply, and Biggles thrust his way into the group in no uncertain manner. For two or three seconds he glared at the aggressors. Then as a uniformed attendant moved towards them he said quietly to Ginger: 'Come on.'

'By gosh! Am I glad to see you?' breathed Ginger fervently, as they walked away. 'I've been tailed ever since I left the Lowenhardts' place.'

'That doesn't greatly surprise me.'

'I gather you got my signal. I expected to find you in Customs.'

By this time they were getting into the car. 'I spotted Molsk and Rallensky outside so I stood back to see who they were waiting for,' explained Biggles. 'I didn't imagine it would be you. They had a nerve, tackling you in the main hall. Were they after something?'

'I have a letter in my pocket addressed to Lowenhardt. The woman at the house let me take it, and I'm afraid the people after me must have worked that out.'

'What's in it?'

'How would I know? It hadn't been opened. The woman in charge of the house told me it arrived just after Lowenhardt had left for England. It bore an English stamp, so thinking it might be important, perhaps having some bearing on the case, I decided to bring it with me if the woman would let me have it. I had a job to persuade her to part with it. In the end Anna's brooch did the trick. Without that I wouldn't have got into the house. I'll hand the letter to Professor Lowenhardt as soon as I see him.'

'You'll be lucky to do that,' said Biggles dryly.

'What do you mean?'

'We haven't seen him and we haven't a clue as to where to look for him. He must have arrived in London before we got your signal.'

'I thought that might happen, but I imagined you'd catch him when he arrived at the house where the Roths are staying. I was sure Anna would give you the address of the place in Hampstead.'

'She did, and a fat lot of good that did us,' returned Biggles bitterly. 'I went along only to discover that the house had been put up for sale six months ago, and nobody knew where Anna's friend, with whom the Roths were to stay, had gone. That knocked all our ideas flat. The man himself, a naturalised German dentist named Jacobs, had lost his wife, fallen sick and retired. Of course, Anna's father can't know that any more than Anna herself did. As soon as I got your signal I sent Algy along to the house to watch for him to arrive and put him wise. He may have gone there, but if so Algy was too late to intercept him. That's how things stand at present.'

'What a blow! What have you done about it?'

'The only thing I could do. There's still a chance that Professor Lowenhardt may go to the house. I mean, he may not have gone straight there when he got off the plane. He may have gone to an hotel to book a room, intending to go on to Hampstead later. That seems to be our only hope. Anyhow, I'm having the house watched until midnight in case he rolls up, By that hour most people are in bed and I wouldn't expect him to call later than that.'

'Who's doing the watching?'

'Bertie is on until nine o'clock, when Algy will take over. He should be on his way there now.'

'Did Bertie see Von Stalhein?'

'He did, and explained the position as far as he knew it at the time. However, Von Stalhein said he'd rather keep out of the way unless there was any particular reason for him to come round. Karkoff and his gang are still eating at the Adlon Restaurant so they can't have made much progress, either.'

'Where's Anna?'

'Still with us. But we can talk about this when we get home. Keep an eye behind us. We may be followed. I'll take a spot of evading action just in case.'

Biggles put his foot down and the car raced on through the falling darkness.

# CHAPTER 8

# ALGY MEETS TROUBLE

BIGGLES and Ginger arrived home without mishap and as far as they were aware without being followed. Living in London they knew the ever-changing one-way streets which so often baffle visitors. They found Bertie and Anna in the sitting-room, a pot of tea and a plate of biscuits on the table.

'Jolly good,' congratulated Bertie, smiling at Ginger. 'So you made it.'

'Just about,' returned Ginger. 'There was a minute when things looked a bit sticky but the army came along and helped me out.'

'Tell us exactly what happened,' requested Biggles, when they had made themselves comfortable. 'But first of all, how did you get on, Bertie? See anything of interest?'

'Not a bally thing. Nobody went to the house while I was there.'

'Algy came along to relieve you as arranged?'

'Dead on time.'

'Good. Now, Ginger, tell us all about it. Things seem to have got into a bit of a tangle so the first thing to do is to try to get some sort of picture of how matters stand at the moment.'

Ginger told the story, in the order of events, of all that

had happened from the time of his arrival in Berlin.

'The woman you saw must have been our house-keeper, Gretchen,' informed Anna, when he had finished. 'She is getting old and cannot really understand all that is going on in our country today. Poor Gretchen. It's hard for the old people.'

'She knows enough to be suspicious of strangers, anyway,' asserted Ginger. 'If it hadn't been for your brooch I should have got nowhere with her. Here it is. You'd better have it back.' He passed it over.

'I should have made allowances for the possibility of the Professor following Anna to London,' muttered Biggles. 'I imagined he might do that but wasn't prepared for him to follow on so soon. Of course, he might have had another reason, apart from Anna, for getting out of Berlin. I wonder was he shadowed when he left the house. In view of what Ginger tells us the house was still being watched. I don't like the sound of that. I can understand the anxiety of the enemy to catch up with the Roths, but what is their interest in your father, Anna? Does he know something, too?'

'Perhaps. It may be that they hope to learn from him where the Roths have gone. Or they may think the Roths will return to Berlin and go to the house.' Anna shrugged. 'I don't know.'

'If your father came here I'm afraid we're going to have a job to find him. Our only chance is that he will go to Doctor Jacobs' old house in Hampstead, if he hasn't already been. I'm not very hopeful but we might catch him there.'

'I'd have thought he'd have gone straight to the house as soon as he arrived,' said Bertie.

'He hadn't been when I called. For all we know he may have had a reason for not going near the house.'

'Such as?'

'He obviously wouldn't go near it if he knew, or suspected, he was being shadowed. No doubt he'd be on the watch for that. His first thought would be to shake off anyone tracking him.'

Bertie nodded. 'I see that.'

'Let's put ourselves in his place,' suggested Biggles. 'Let's assume he went to the house in Bishop's Way. The woman who now lives there would tell him, as she told me, that Doctor Jacobs no longer lived there. She advised me to make inquiries at the estate agent from whom she bought the place, so it's reasonable to suppose she'd offer the same advice to the Professor. Very well. Let us suppose, since there was nothing else he could do, that he went to the agent, bearing in mind that by this time he'd be sick with worry wondering where Anna had gone. The agent spoke freely to me because I'm a police officer, but he may not have said so much to the Professor. But that isn't the point. When I left the agent I asked him to let me know if anyone called making inquiries about Doctor Jacobs. He said he would. I haven't heard from him, and that can only mean one of two things. Either the Professor has not yet been to the house where Doctor Jacobs lived, or if he has, he has not been to the estate agent. Looked at like that there would seem to be a fair chance of our finding him in Hampstead.'

Everyone agreed.

'In the meantime,' said Ginger, taking the letter addressed to the Professor from his pocket and laying it on the table, 'what are we going to do about this?'

Biggles picked up the envelope and examined it closely, without comment, before passing it on to Anna.

'Does that handwriting mean anything to you?' he questioned.

Anna studied the address. 'It is something like the writing of Doctor Jacobs, but I wouldn't be sure of it. I used to see it often when I lived with the family, but that was some time ago. If it is his writing it has changed.'

'He may have tried to disguise it.'

'Perhaps. But it is more like the writing of a child.'

'The Doctor has aged since you knew him, and he has been ill.'

Anna shook her head. 'I don't know.'

'Can you think of anyone else in England who might write to your father?'

'No.'

'The trouble is I can't read the postmark,' complained Biggles. 'Someone banged it on in a hurry and only caught one corner. Queer how often that happens when you have a reason for wanting to read the postmark. I'd say the letter was posted somewhere outside London. You'd better take charge of it, Anna. What it contains may have no bearing on the present situation, but, on the other hand, it could answer some of the questions that have got us guessing.'

Anna looked dubious. 'I don't think I should open a letter addressed to someone else, even to my father.'

'I shan't try to persuade you to. That's a matter between you and your conscience. In the ordinary way the question would never arise, but here the circumstances are far from ordinary. It's just possible that the lives of your father and your friends could depend on the contents of this letter, and I'm bound to point out that if you discovered that too late you'd never forgive yourself.'

'That's as good as saying you think I should open it.'

'Frankly, I don't see how it could do any harm. As our concern is only for the safety of your father and the Roths it would be pardonable. But, as I say, it's a matter for you to decide. I wouldn't open it myself, but you, after all, are the Professor's daughter, and that's a very different matter. All I ask is, whatever you do, don't carry that letter about with you.'

'I could leave it in my bedroom.'

'I don't know that it would be entirely safe there. We're dealing with an unscrupulous gang of ruffians who stop at nothing. Rather than risk losing the letter it would be better to destroy it. Imagine how you would feel if your enemies got hold of it and it turned out to contain vital information.'

Anna was looking really worried. She thought for a moment or two, all eyes on her. 'I am in your hands,' she said at last. 'I will do whatever you advise.'

Biggles smiled reproachfully. 'That's putting the onus on me. Very well. My advice to you is this. Open the letter and read it. If the contents have nothing to do with us you need say nothing more about it. Do what you like with it. Burn it, or keep it and give it to your father when we find him. If it should give a clue to the whereabouts of your father, the Roths, or Doctor Jacobs, I'd be glad to have it.'

'I will open it,' decided Anna. 'I am fearful for my father.'

With hands that were trembling slightly she picked up a knife from the table, slit the flap of the envelope and took out a single sheet of notepaper folded once across. Unfolding it she first turned it over to look at the signature. She looked up. 'It's from —'

At that moment the door was thrown open and into the room, somewhat unsteadily, came Algy. That something had happened to him was at once evident. His hair was ruffled and his face pale. There was a red bruise on one cheek. His collar was torn open with a tie, hanging loose, on one side. His left hand was heavily bandaged.

Everyone stared. Biggles, who had leapt to his feet on Algy's sudden entry, remained standing. 'How did you get in that mess?' he asked sharply.

Algy, who had crossed the room to an armchair, sank heavily into it. 'Give me a drink,' he requested.

'Give him a nip of brandy,' Biggles told Ginger. Then, to Algy: 'Are you badly hurt? Shall I send for the doctor?'

'I've had one, thanks,' replied Algy, smiling bleakly. 'No, I'm all right. Just give me a minute.' He took a gulp from the glass Ginger handed to him. 'Ah! That's better.'

Said Biggles, after a pause. 'Have you seen Professor Lowenhardt?'

'I – er – think so.'

'You only think! Don't you know?'

'As I've never seen him in my life how could I be sure? Besides, it was dark. But I think it must have been him.'

'Where is he now?'

'I don't know.'

Biggles drew a deep breath. He sat down. 'All right,' he said. 'When you're ready tell us about it.'

Algy finished the brandy. 'That won't take long.'

With everyone waiting, after a brief silence he went on. 'It happened so quickly that it was all over before I realised it had begun. I took over from Bertie as arranged. Just before ten o'clock it got chilly. Then it started to rain. There didn't seem to be any reason, with another two hours to do, why I should stand there getting wet through.'

'Where were you standing?'

'Against a garden wall on the other side of the road, not quite opposite. The street lighting wasn't all that good, but from there I'd be able to see anyone going to Westwinds. Deciding I could do the job more comfortably I went to the junction of Bishop's Way and the main road and picked up a taxi. I agreed to pay the driver waiting time and he took me back to my original position, tight in against the kerb. All lights were switched off except the cab's sidelights.'

'You were on the far side of the road, not quite opposite Westwinds?'

'Exactly. It seemed the best position. No one could see me sitting in the cab. There was very little traffic and few pedestrians, as you'd expect on a wet night.'

'Carry on.'

'About half an hour later I saw a man coming along the pavement, from the direction of the main road, on the same side as the house I was watching. Two or three times he stopped, looking at the houses as if trying to make out the names or numbers. His general behaviour was that of a stranger trying to locate a particular address. Naturally, this made me sit up and take notice. I had a feeling he was going to stop at Number eleven, Westwinds, and he did. With a hand on the gate he had a good look up and down the street.' Algy smiled ruefully.

'I suppose you might say I was partly to blame for what followed,' he went on. 'I can see that now. But as you can imagine my entire attention was on the man at the gate, and I didn't see the other two until they jumped him. Neither, I'm sure, did he, or he wouldn't have

T–D

stood there as he did. Where they came from I don't
know, but they must have been following him. I had
already opened the door of the taxi, my intention being
to walk over and introduce myself. I didn't want to
appear in too much of a hurry for fear of giving the man
a fright. It was at that moment the other two appeared
and went for him. I let out a shout and dashed across the
road. I'm not quite clear about what happened after
that. I grabbed one of the men by the arms whereupon
the other fetched me a wallop in the face. Then the taxi
driver arrived on the scene and he really sailed in. I must
say he was a stout feller. After all, it wasn't his fight, but
he behaved as if it was. He fairly let 'em have it. I don't
suppose the affair lasted more than a minute but by that
time the two toughs had had enough, and bolted. When I
looked round for the man they'd attacked he wasn't
there. I don't know which way he went. I didn't see him
go. He didn't make a sound and I never really saw his
face. I'd been too busy to look at him. I suddenly came
over a bit faint. I didn't know why till my taxi pal said,
"My Gawd! They've sliced you." Then I saw my hand
was bleeding pretty badly, apparently from a knife
wound. The driver, a local man, whisked me round to
the hospital where it needed five stitches to sew me up.
He waited and afterwards brought me home.'

'I hope you gave him a jolly good tip,' said Bertie.

'You bet I did. Well, that's about all.'

'Tell me this,' said Biggles. 'Did you get a good look
at the men?'

'No. They wore raincoats with the collars turned
up and had mufflers over the lower parts of their
faces.'

'You couldn't say if they were some of Karkoff's
gang?'

'No. They might have been, but I wouldn't swear to it either way.'

'How are you feeling now?'

'I'm all right.'

Biggles lit a cigarette. 'It must have been Anna's father who went to the house. He may have suspected he was being followed. Maybe that's why he left it until after dark before going to Hampstead. Pity you couldn't have made contact with him, but things might have been worse. No doubt they would have been worse had you not been there. You couldn't do more than you did. There is this about it.' Biggles looked at Anna. 'If we don't know where your father is neither do the people who had been following him.'

'I don't understand,' answered Anna, who naturally was looking upset. 'If they wanted to kill him why did they wait until he was outside the house?'

'They didn't want to kill him – not before then, anyway. I imagine the people they are really after are the Roths, and they were shadowing your father hoping he'd lead them to where they were staying, which is exactly what he did, or would have done had the Roths been at Westwinds. The position as it now stands looks like this. The hoodlums who are after the Roths must think they know where they're staying. Actually, as we know, they're wrong. They still no more know where the Roths are at this moment than we do. Unfortunately the same thing applies to your father. He doesn't know that Doctor Jacobs has moved, or that the Roths are not where he thinks they are.'

'What a terrible muddle,' murmured Anna. 'What do you think my father will do?'

'We might as well face it. After what has happened tonight he'll be more worried than ever, afraid that he's given away the Roths' hiding-place. Actually, as we know, he has not; but in his anxiety the most natural thing for him to do would be to make another attempt to get in touch with the Roths to warn them of their danger – that their enemies know where they are, as he supposes.'

'You think he'll go back to Westwinds.'

'Not necessarily. Assuming the house will be watched he may try another method of communication. He might write a letter and either post it or employ an express messenger boy to deliver it. But whatever he does, even if he should get a message through the result will confuse him. A letter addressed to Doctor Jacobs would almost certainly be returned marked not known. The Mrs Smith who now lives in the house knows nothing of Doctor Jacobs. If she passed the letter to the house agent he wouldn't be able to do anything with it because he has no idea of where the Doctor has gone.'

'What about the telephone?' queried Ginger.

'If Mrs Smith has kept it on it will be in her name; which means the telephone directory would be useless.'

'My father may have kept a note of Doctor Jacobs' number,' said Anna.

'What would he make of it when he was answered by a woman named Smith who would say she knew nothing of Doctor Jacobs? That was the answer I got when I called, and no doubt the answer the Karkoff gang will get should they go there.'

'Then what are we going to do?'

Biggles shook his head. 'London is a big place to start looking for anyone. I'll think about it. All we can do at present is keep watch on the house in Bishop's Way in case your father should go there again.'

'I'll go and watch,' declared Anna. 'I shall know him if he comes.'

'And those men who followed you from Berlin will know *you*, should they come along, as they probably will. No, Anna, I wouldn't advise that. But what about this letter? You were just going to read it when Algy came in. You might as well do that; then, as it's getting late, Bertie will see you to your hotel.'

Anna picked up the letter. 'It's from Doctor Jacobs,' she announced.

'Doctor Jacobs!' exclaimed Biggles. 'Why didn't you say so? We've been sitting here . . . but I'm sorry. Go on. What does he say?'

'He writes in German so I will translate as I go,' resumed Anna, and read aloud: 'My dear friend, this is to tell you that should you or Anna come to London you will not find me at the old address in Hampstead. Some time ago, having no one but myself to think of, and not being in good health, I decided to retire and spend my last days in the peace and quiet of the country. I found such a place near the village of Saxton, in Sussex, from where I now write. I did not write earlier because I had in mind to see Berlin once more before I die, when I would give myself the pleasure of exchanging news with you. But now I read of the troubles in Berlin I think it better that I should remember it as it was in the happy days when we were boys together. Instead, I write this letter. Should you or Anna come to England I would be overjoyed to see you. I have plenty of room. This house is larger than the one I thought to have but I fell in love with the garden and because it is in the country I could buy it cheaply. Give my love to dear Anna. Always affectionately yours, Bruno." '

'So now we know,' said Biggles. 'Where is this house?'

Anna read the address. 'Saxton Old Hall, near Saxton, Sussex.'

'Well, that answers two questions for us. At least we know where the Doctor can be found.'

'And the other?'

'We have found a home for you.'

Anna looked surprised. 'For me?'

'Why not? A temporary home, anyway. What better place could you find?'

'But I couldn't leave London without knowing where my father —'

Biggles raised a hand. 'Let's not argue about it now. It's getting late. We can talk about it in the morning. You settle up at the hotel and pack your case ready for Saxton.'

Ginger spoke. 'All I can say is, it's a good thing I didn't leave that letter in Berlin.'

'What a pity my father just missed it,' said Anna sadly.

'I'd say it's just as well,' Biggles told her seriously. 'Had he read that letter he would have gone straight to Saxton and arrived with enemies hard on his heels. Then anything could have happened.'

'Yes. I didn't think of that,' agreed Anna.

'That's enough for today,' concluded Biggles, getting up. 'Bertie, you might call a cab and see Anna home.'

# CHAPTER 9

# ANNA DISOBEYS ORDERS

THE following morning at breakfast Biggles announced that he had decided definitely to take Anna to Saxton, and if Doctor Jacobs would have her leave her there. They could not, he asserted, keep her shut up in the hotel, and to let her wander about the streets without an escort might be dangerous. There was no purpose in it, anyway. He felt sure that when Doctor Jacobs knew what had happened he would take good care of her. The car was outside ready.

He had just got up from the table when the phone rang. He took the call, and listened for some time, saying little. Once he grimaced at the others as if to prepare them for bad news. At length he hung up.

'Who on earth was that, at this hour?' asked Algy.

'Carson, the estate agent who handled the sale of the house for Doctor Jacobs. He said he was wondering if I'd heard what happened at Westwinds last night or early this morning. Naturally, I thought he meant the affair in which you were involved, but it wasn't that at all. It seems the house was broken into. Mrs Smith was knocked unconscious. She's been taken to hospital where a police officer is waiting for her to come round.

The police are puzzled because nothing in the house appears to have been touched. That's the local gossip, anyhow.'

'Who discovered this?'

'The milkman. He saw the door had been forced open. He looked inside and saw Mrs Smith on the floor, in her nightdress. It looks as if she heard a noise, went down to investigate and was knocked on the head. Anna's father would have no reason to do that. We can guess who did. They didn't lose much time. What a confounded nuisance. This upsets all my plans for the day, apart from raising an awkward situation.'

'Why should it?'

'Use your head. The local police are on the job. We can't withhold what we know about it. It means I shall have to go round. The problem will be how much to say. They may have found finger-prints. If so I shall have to say I may know who made them. Again, what if Professor Lowenhardt goes back to the house? They'd probably take him to the police station for questioning. I shall have to tell them about him and do my best to explain that the thing is probably a case of mistaken identity. The men who broke into the house were looking for some people they thought were there. I shall have to go to Hampstead. One of you will have to go to the office and let the Chief know what's cooking; and I'd planned to keep the house in Bishop's Way watched in case the Professor —'

Biggles broke off as the phone rang again. 'Stiffen the crows! What's going on this morning,' he muttered irritably, as he picked up the receiver. Again he listened, but this time the call did not last as long. All he said was: 'Thanks. Much obliged.' Leaving the instrument he walked to the window and looked down into the street.

'Now what?' prompted Ginger.

Biggles lit a cigarette and tossed the match impatiently into the ash-tray. 'More cheerful news. We're being watched. That was Von Stalhein on the phone, speaking from a call-box. He was on his way here to have a word with Anna when he spotted a car parked on the opposite side of the road. A grey Vauxhall. He's seen it outside the Adlon Restaurant and the Cosmolite Hotel. It belongs to Karkoff. Von Stalhein thought he'd better keep clear, but he tipped me off in case I didn't know. He's right. The car's still there. I've just seen it.'

'But that's absurd,' protested Algy. 'How could Karkoff or his gang know anything about us or that we lived here?'

Biggles sat down and drew heavily on his cigarette. 'We may have underestimated them. I can think of one way they might have tracked us here, although until now the chance would have seemed remote. Last night, Algy, you told us that after the scrap in Bishop's Way the two men made off.'

'That's right. What about it?'

'I have an idea they didn't go far. They must have seen your taxi standing there and from the way you jumped out realised you'd been watching the house. You say you didn't see them again?'

'I didn't look for them. I was more concerned with the man they'd attacked, presumably the Professor.'

'I can understand that. They may have had a car handy. They could have picked up a taxi. If so there was nothing to prevent them from following you here.'

'Why tail me? Why should they?'

'Use your head. Look at the whole affair as we have reason to understand it. The Professor must have been

shadowed from the moment he left his house in Berlin,
apparently in the hope that he would lead the way to
where the Roths were hiding – which in fact, as far as he
knew, he did. That was all the men following him
wanted to know. Why they attacked him I don't know,
but the intention may have been to knock him out and
then go into the house to deal with the Roths. Be that as
it may, their scheme came unstuck when you barged in.
It stands to reason they'd want to know who you were
and what your game was. They'd have to know for their
own security. The only way they could get that information would be by following you home. I'd wager
that's what happened. Now they're watching the house
to find out more about you.'

'Don't forget I went to the hospital.'

'What difference would that make? Your taxi waited
for you. They'd take up the trail again when you came
out. These butchers must be expert at this sort of thing.
It's their job, and their lives depend on doing it
thoroughly. I'm mighty grateful to Von Stalhein for letting us know about that car outside because I wouldn't
have suspected it, and had I started for Saxton with
Anna I'd have played right into their hands. Which
shows how careful we've got to be.'

'So what do we do now?'

'As they've only one car they can't follow us all if we
go separate ways. I'd rather Algy wasn't seen because he
might be recognised as the man who butted in last night.
Bertie, this is where you take the car and lay a false trail
to get that Vauxhall out of the way. I shall then go to
Hampstead. Ginger, you'll get another car from the Yard
garage and take Anna to Saxton. I've no idea where the
place is so look it up on the map. Before you start ring
Anna at the hotel to make sure she's all ready to move

off, her bill paid and her case packed. Say you'll be along for her in about half an hour. That should give you time to fetch a car from the garage.'

Ginger fetched a pair of binoculars and focused them on the Vauxhall. 'Two men in the front seats,' he observed. 'I wouldn't swear to it but they look like Rallensky and Molsk.'

'That's what I'd expect,' said Biggles. 'The man who tailed you from Berlin may have returned to Germany. Or, of course, he may have joined forces with Karkoff. But never mind that. Ring Anna to tell her to get ready.'

Ginger was reaching for the phone when the door opened and Anna, carrying her case, walked in. 'Good morning,' she greeted with a bright smile.

Biggles did not return it. Looking as if he had received a mortal wound he let out a sigh that was almost a groan. 'We just needed this,' he breathed. With a grim expression he regarded the cheerful face of their visitor. 'Didn't I tell you not on any account to leave the hotel?' he inquired sternly.

'Yes ... but ...'

'Don't make excuses. You're a very naughty girl. You've upset all my plans.'

Anna stared. She had never seen Biggles in this mood.

'But I know the way. It's only a short distance. I thought my coming round would save you the trouble —'

'Never mind what you thought, Anna. No doubt you acted for the best. You might have been killed, or kidnapped. That may still happen. You must learn to obey orders.'

'But I didn't see anyone —'

'If you look out of the window you will see a grey motor-car. In it are the men who hope to murder your friends, the Roths. They must have seen you arrive so they know where you are. I was going to take you to Saxton where you would be safe with Doctor Jacobs. How am I going to get you there now without being followed? That is one thing. Another is, the house where Doctor Jacobs used to live was broken into early this morning and the unfortunate woman who lives there is in hospital seriously injured.'

Anna looked as if she was going to burst into tears, but she recovered.

'I can only say I am very sorry,' she said contritely.

'I'm sure you are, but that doesn't mend the mischief. Whatever we do that car will wait until you come out and follow you. I must go to Hampstead in case your father returns to Westwinds. How are we going to get you away from here without being seen? That's our problem now.'

'I don't understand all this following,' said Anna, shaking her head. 'Why does anyone follow me? I have done nothing.'

'Very well. Let me try to make the position clear, starting from the beginning with Herr Roth, who until recently occupied an official post behind the Iron Curtain but apparently was no longer trusted; so he was arrested and shot. Certain papers were missing. His home was searched but they were not found. No doubt the Roth family would have been arrested had they not fled. We may suppose the house was searched again after they had gone. As nothing was found it became necessary to find the Roths who by this time had taken refuge with you and your father in West Berlin. You follow me so far?'

'Yes.'

'How the East German secret police knew the Roths were friendly with you I don't know, but it seems likely that Herr Roth had been watched for some time and his visits to you in the Antonstrasse noted. It might have been known that you were engaged to Moritz. Spies have a way of learning such things. Be that as it may, your house would naturally fall under suspicion of having given shelter to the Roths, so it was watched. You would know where the Roths had gone. That was why you, and later your father, were followed to England. It was hoped you would reveal where the Roths were hiding, and as a matter of fact you would have done that had I not intervened. Your father would have done it, too, had Doctor Jacobs not left Hampstead.'

Anna nodded. 'Yes, I see that.'

Biggles continued. 'In the meantime three men had been sent here from East Germany to silence the Roths, or recover the missing documents – perhaps both. In my opinion these men were not particularly concerned with you or your father in the first instance. It's the Roths they're after, and you, by helping them, have become involved. No doubt the enemy agents still believe you know where the Roths are hiding. Your father was followed to Hampstead. Now, having satisfied themselves that the Roths are not at the house in Bishop's Way they must be wondering why he went there. Unfortunately, it now seems that after the fight there last night Algy was followed back here, with the result that we, too, are now being watched from a car parked outside. You have played into their hands by coming here. They still hope you'll lead them to the Roths, and unless we can find a way to outwit them they'll never stop

following you until you do. That's how things stand at
this moment. Now do you understand?'

'I think so. But what about my father?'

'After last night he'll realise he was followed and, if
he's wise, go into hiding. It's unlikely the enemy will
find him and we haven't time to look for him now. The
first thing we have to do is get you into the safe keeping
of Doctor Jacobs. That will leave us free to look for
your father, and the Roths. The immediate problem is
how to get you away from here without being seen.'

Bertie spoke. 'What you mean, old boy, is this. If I go
off in the car they won't follow me?'

'Not now they know Anna is here. They may or may
not know who we are or how we come into this, but as
Anna has come to England they'll reckon she's certain
to know where the Roths are. Obviously, she's the one
to shadow.'

'I could get my own car out and block the Vauxhall
from getting away.'

'That wouldn't really solve our problem. You
couldn't keep that up indefinitely and they'd still be able
to see what went on here.'

Ginger came into the argument. 'We could prevent
that. You want a taxi to go to Hampstead. Algy will
need one to go to the office and report to the Chief. You
and Algy could go round to the garage, hire two cabs
and fix it with the drivers to pull in tight against the
Vauxhall to block its view. You can't see over the top of
a regulation taxi. Bertie then shoots off in the car. As
soon as the Vauxhall can get clear it'll follow him.'

'Why should it?'

'Because seeing that Anna is in neither of the taxis
it'll be supposed she's in it.'

'It won't take 'em long to discover she isn't.'

'Maybe not; but by the time they've done that and come back Anna could be away. You could have taken us round to the garage where, if Bertie doesn't mind, we could borrow his Jaguar and press on to Saxton.'

'It might work,' assented Biggles. 'No harm in trying. We shall have to do something. We've lost too much time already. Let's have a bash at it. I'll go round with Algy to get the cabs. The rest of you stand by to move fast when we come back. Bertie, have a couple of over-coats ready to stick up in the back seat of the car as if it might be Anna trying to hide. We should be back inside ten minutes. Come on, Algy, let's get on with it.'

They went off.

The others watched the grey car from the window. It did not move.

'Biggles was right,' said Bertie. 'They're not going to budge until they see Anna come out.' He fetched an overcoat and a travelling rug. With these over his arm they went to the front door from where Ginger watched events through the letter-box.

They had not long to wait. The two cabs came round the corner in close touch. The drivers had evidently been well briefed, for they played their part with perfect precision, pulling up, almost touching, tight against the Vauxhall, blocking its view.

'This is it,' snapped Ginger, throwing open the door.

Bertie dashed out, piled his load in the back seat of the car high against the window, slipped into the driving-seat and was off, accelerating.

The Vauxhall, risking grazed paintwork, extricated itself and set off in pursuit. In a minute both cars were out of sight. Ginger and Anna crossed the road quickly and got into Biggles' taxi.

'Back to the garage,' Biggles told his driver.

The rest was easy. Ginger and Anna had only to get into Bertie's Jaguar, and after a last word with Biggles set a course for Saxton, the locality of which he had checked on the AA map.

The weather was fine, and, as a matter of detail, Ginger was looking forward to the drive. After all, a run into the country with a pretty girl did not come his way every day.

It turned out to be as pleasant as he anticipated. There was not much conversation and this was almost entirely confined to the problems still to be solved – how the Roths were to be found, and, of course, Anna's father who, naturally, was uppermost in her mind. Ginger kept an eye on the road behind him, but as far as he could make out he was not being followed. Nor, after the manner in which they had got away, did he expect to be.

After a break at a wayside tavern for a cup of coffee, and another look at the map, an hour later saw them cruising through the tranquil hamlet of Saxton, with its old Norman church tower standing four square to the winds of heaven. A road worker directed them to the Old Hall, half a mile beyond the village, on the left-hand side, standing in its own grounds.

Ginger went on, confident now that he had nothing to worry about.

This happy frame of mind did not last long.

Just before he reached the gate that marked the entrance to the drive that led to the house he had a second look at a car standing half on the verge, facing the village – that is, on its right side of the road. The bonnet was propped open and a man appeared to be doing something to the engine. With his head bent low over it, it was not possible to see his face.

'Why did you look so hard at that man?' asked Anna curiously.

'In my work one gets in the habit of looking hard at anything that doesn't entirely add up to normal,' answered Ginger casually as he allowed the car to slow down.

'Was there anything about the man that didn't quite add up, as you call it?'

'Nothing worth talking about. Maybe as things are I'm inclined to be a bit sensitive and over-suspicious. That fellow's suit was made of a cloth few Englishmen would wear. I've nothing against it but I doubt if it was made in this country.'

'But many foreigners come here.'

'True enough. But that car looked like a brand new Triumph Herald. Why should the engine be giving trouble? And if there's something seriously wrong why didn't the man stop me to ask if I could help, or leave a message at the next garage? That would be usual.'

Anna looked at Ginger sideways. 'How you notice little things.'

'I wouldn't be much good at my job if I didn't. Often it's the little things that count.'

'You don't think – the man – could be watching – the house we're going to?'

'I wouldn't think so.'

'Those nasty people who have been following me couldn't possibly know that Doctor Jacobs lives here. That's impossible.'

'I used to talk like that but after one or two sharp lessons I'm careful how I use the word impossible.'

By this time the Jaguar was crawling up a badly rutted gravel drive between an area of overgrown flowering shrubs, rhododendrons and the like, to a house of some size, obviously old although of no particular period. An attempt had been made to tidy up the garden but it was still largely a jungle of weeds.

Ginger pulled up at the front door. 'You might as well sit where you are until I've made sure the Doctor is at home,' he told Anna, as he got out. There was no bell so he knocked.

There was no answer.

'I'm afraid there's no one at home,' he said as he knocked again.

'There's someone in the house,' advised Anna. 'I saw a curtain move at one of the upstairs windows.'

'Then get out and show yourself. The Doctor should recognise you. Perhaps he doesn't like strangers.'

Anna stepped out and looked up at the window. Ginger knocked again.

Presently there came the sounds of a lock being turned and bolts being drawn. The door was opened a few inches and a middle-aged woman in a nurse's uniform regarded them coldly. 'What do you want?' she asked.

'I believe Doctor Jacobs lives here,' answered Ginger somewhat disconcerted by this uncivil reception. 'I've brought a friend to see him. I hope he isn't ill.'

'Tell him it's Anna Lowenhardt,' put in Anna.

'I will tell him,' said the woman, closing the door and locking it.

Ginger shrugged. 'Looks as if the Doctor is nervous about something,' he observed.

The woman came back. Looking at Anna she said: 'Come with me.' To Ginger she added: 'You can wait here.'

Anna went in. The door was closed and again locked. Ginger strolled to the car and leaned against it prepared to wait. He had no alternative and could only hope he wouldn't be kept hanging about for too long. Knowing Biggles would be anxious to have his report he wanted to get back to London, but he could hardly leave things as they were. Anna's case was still in the car, anyway.

He had stood there for some time thinking of nothing in particular when a slight movement, where everything else was still, drew his eyes to the spot, some twenty yards or so down the drive. As it occurred in some evergreen shrubs it might have been a bird, and that was what he thought had caused the movement of the leaves at a spot five or six feet from the ground. His nerves twitched when he made out a face looking at him from between some twigs. Even as he looked there was another slight movement as the leaves, which had evidently been drawn aside, were allowed to settle back into their proper position, hiding the face.

Ginger gave no indication that he had seen what he had seen. His gaze wandered away from the spot, his elbow on the bonnet of the car and his chin in his hand. He yawned, and presently half turned his back. But his brain was racing. Clearly, someone was watching him, or the house; it didn't matter which. Either way it was something he had not reckoned on, or even imagined might happen. His first sensation was shock. Then, as this passed, he began to wonder what he should do about it. He would have to do something. He couldn't go back to London and leave things like this. All his plans, such as they were, collapsed.

How long had this been going on? was one of the first thoughts to occur to him. Did Doctor Jacobs know his house was being watched? Was that why the woman who had answered the door had been so offhand? Possibly. In fact, very probably. Biggles would have to know about it and the sooner the better. How could he do that? If there was a telephone in the house it should be easy. If not . . . how? What on earth was Anna doing, keeping him waiting all this time. The sooner she knew what was going on —

The door was opened and Anna appeared. 'The Doctor would like to talk to you,' she announced cheerfully.

'And I want to talk to him,' returned Ginger grimly.

'Will you bring my case, please? I'm going to stay here.'

Ginger collected the case and followed Anna into the house.

# CHAPTER 10

# A SHOCK FOR BIGGLES

As soon as Ginger and Anna were away in Bertie's car Biggles instructed the driver of his taxi to take him to the house at Hampstead where Doctor Jacobs had once lived. Exactly what he would do and say he did not know; that, he had decided, could be left until he had seen the officer in charge of the investigations into the attack on Mrs Smith. He was prepared for a difficult situation, at all events until he had explained his interest, because he was not known in that particular Police Division, and local officers might resent interference from Scotland Yard unless its assistance had been called for. Tact would be needed.

Actually, Biggles would have preferred to keep away from the house, but dare not take the risk of missing Professor Lowenhardt should he return to it. Aside from that he was anxious to know what the police had made of the case, if they had found any clues. And, of course, he felt bound to tell them what he knew.

In the event, however, any early objections to his intrusion were soon ironed out.

Telling his taxi to wait he found a police constable on duty at the door with orders to admit no one, this applying particularly to newspaper reporters. Inside, he was told on showing his credentials, conducting the

117

inquiry were Chief Superintendent Lowe and the station sergeant. He sent in his name with the result that he was admitted.

The Chief Superintendent regarded him, if not with disapproval, then without enthusiasm. 'What brings you here?' he inquired. 'I'll send for the Yard when I'm ready. I can handle this.'

'I'm sure you can, Chief,' returned Biggles evenly. 'I don't want to barge in, believe me, but I had to come along because I'm sure I can help you.'

'You mean you've got a theory about what's happened here?' The Chief was still slightly cynical.

'I've more than a theory. I have some facts which, when you've heard them, you'll agree I could hardly have withheld.'

'What sort of facts?'

'For instance, I know who broke in here, and why.'

The Chief stared. 'How the hell —'

'To save you time I've come to tell you what I know. That's all. It's a queer business and involves factors you couldn't possibly suspect. If you'll listen I'll tell you what they are, afterwards leaving it to your discretion what you do about them. Before I start I want you to tell me one thing. Has a man named Professor Lowenhardt been here this morning?'

'Not to my knowledge. Who's he? I've never heard of him.'

'You wouldn't, unless he had been here. I'm desperately anxious to get in touch with him. He came here about midnight and would have been murdered had I not had a man watching the house. But I'll come to that presently. Where Mrs Smith is concerned I have no interest. The attack on her was a case of mistaken identity.'

'That could explain why I'm not making much progress,' admitted the Chief. 'Nothing appears to have been touched so I was stuck for a motive.'

'Any finger-prints?'

'Not so far.'

'All right. This is the story. It'll take a minute or two to tell so we might as well sit down.' Biggles lit a cigarette.

'Do you really mean you know the name of the man who broke in here and coshed Mrs Smith?' asked the Chief, almost incredulously.

'There were probably two men at least, since they came to commit murder – probably a triple murder.'

'For God's sake! Would I be likely to know them?'

'No. They're professional killers who recently came to this country with orders to bump off certain people. Mrs Smith was not one of them. The wretched woman must have got in the way. What I'm going to tell you is strictly under the hat. If one squeak gets out these murdering hounds may still get away with what they came to do, and then slip out of the country without us being able to do anything about it.'

'I'd see about that,' swore the Chief.

Biggles shook his head sadly. 'Why do you suppose I haven't done anything about it? This is a political job, and these swine are in the happy position of being able to take cover under diplomatic immunity. You'll see more clearly what I mean in a minute.'

Biggles went on to explain the escape of the Roth family from Germany, how they were being hunted by East German agents and why it was thought they were in the house supposedly occupied by Doctor Jacobs. He touched on the arrival of Professor Lowenhardt who had come to warn them, how he had been followed and had managed to escape. 'Karkoff's killers must have come back here afterwards, imagining the Roths were inside, to finish the job,' he concluded. 'Frankly, I wasn't prepared for them to strike again so quickly as that or I'd have been here. As I see it now perhaps I should have warned Mrs Smith of what might happen, but I couldn't see the immediate necessity of upsetting her.'

'She must have heard a noise as the devils broke in and came down to see what was going on.'

'That's what happened, without a doubt.'

'The silly woman should have dialled 999. We'd have been here inside five minutes.'

'Perhaps she couldn't get to the phone. Anyway, there it is. My angle is simply to prevent these unfortunate German refugees from being murdered. Just that and no more. The girl Anna is now on her way to Doctor Jacobs where she should be safe. My next job is to find her father. He doesn't know Jacobs has moved and must still be under the impression that he lives in this house. And, of course, I'm anxious to locate the Roths. They know Jacobs doesn't live here any more but they can't have any idea of where he's living now.'

'Are you sure of that?'

'Yes. Mrs Smith told me, when I came here, that three people answering to the description of the Roths had called. She told them Jacobs no longer lived here; she knew nothing about him.'

'You say you know where these thugs hang out?' prompted the Chief.

'Yes. Anyhow, until yesterday they were living at the Cosmolite Hotel, in the Cromwell Road, Kensington.'

'And there's nothing you can do about 'em?'

'Not a thing as long as they behave themselves.'

'I wouldn't call what they did here behaving themselves.'

'How are you going to prove they did it? You say you haven't a clue, not even a finger-print. You get a line on them, hooking them up with what's happened here, and I'll see they don't get into any more mischief – for a time, anyway.'

'Would it suit you to have 'em picked up on suspicion?'

'Certainly. But what grounds have you for that?'

'A check on their papers might reveal a flaw. If they weren't in order we might get 'em out of the country on a deporation order, as dangerous aliens.'

'That could serve for the moment, but it wouldn't solve my problem in the long run.'

'Why not?'

'Being what they are, professional agents in state employment, it's a thousand to one they will have been provided with papers in perfect order. Even if we did find something wrong, and picked them up, they'd simply be replaced by another gang. You know the old saying, better the devil you know than one you don't know.'

'Yes. I suppose you're right. Well, what are you going to do about it?'

'Somehow, I don't know how, I've got to find Professor Lowenhardt, and the Roths, and get them somewhere reasonably safe. The present situation has boiled up by the unfortunate circumstance of Doctor Jacobs having moved. I shall be interested to know what *you* decide to do about it. Don't for heaven's sake let a word of this get into the newspapers; that won't make things any easier for either of us.'

'I'll see that doesn't happen,' promised the Chief. 'I

may still find something here. I haven't finished yet.'

'All right. That suits me. You might let me know if Lowenhardt turns up, or anything else of importance. You'll get me, or one of my assistants, at the Yard, or my home address. Here's my number. I'll tell you if anything happens at my end. I felt I had to tell you what I knew about this.'

'Thanks. I'm glad you did. Queer business. I knew Doctor Jacobs pretty well.'

Biggles looked surprised. 'Oh. How did that come about?'

'As you know, he was a German by birth, naturalised British. He came here before the war. Naturally, when the war broke out, and the panic flared up about spies, he was put on the list of possible fifth columnists working for Hitler. I was a sergeant at the time and took part in the general round-up.'

'Was Jacobs arrested?'

'No. As a matter of fact he wasn't. His record was good. As a top dental surgeon he was well known in the profession, doing a lot of useful work, some of it in military hospitals. Several of our doctors were prepared to stand guarantee for him, and he was, after all, a Jew who had left Germany to escape Nazi persecution. So we merely kept an eye on him and let it go at that. He was all right. I knew he had left the district but I had no idea where he went. I had no occasion to get in touch with him, but I could have got his address had I wanted it.'

Biggles looked up sharply. 'You could?'

'Of course.'

'How?'

'As a Doctor of Dental Surgery no doubt the professional societies would be in contact with him if only to forward the latest papers and periodicals. Even after retirement I imagine he'd want to keep up to date with the work he'd been doing all his life. No doubt I could have got his address through them.'

Biggles bit his lip. 'I didn't think of that. I seem to have slipped up there. Not that I had much time to think about it. You've got me worried. If you could have got Jacobs' address through his profession no doubt other people could have done it.'

'I suppose so.'

'Hm. That gives me another worry.'

At this juncture the telephone rang. The Chief Superintendent answered it. He handed the receiver to Biggles saying: 'It's for you.'

Biggles took over and listened. All he said was: 'All right. Stay where you are. I'm on my way.' Having replaced the receiver, speaking to Chief Superintendent he went on: 'I shall have to go. That call was from the Yard. It seems as if one of my lads is in trouble. I'll be seeing you again. If Professor Lowenhardt should come back here you might tell him to report to my office at the Yard and wait for me there. Someone will be on duty. Better still, if you have transport available, in order to make sure he doesn't get a knife in his back I'd be obliged if you'd arrange for one of your cars to take him. The same with the Roths, although I doubt if they'll return. Goodness only knows what's happened to them.'

'Meanwhile if I can get a line on these crooks for what they've done here I shall pick them up.'

'Of course. I shall breathe more freely if I know they're out of circulation. So long.'

He went out and in a minute was on his way to Headquarters.

On arrival he made his way quickly to the office where he found Algy and Bertie waiting for him. 'All right, go ahead and give me the gen,' he requested tersely. 'What's this about Ginger?'

'I took the call from him – Bertie hadn't come in then,' answered Algy. 'He rang from the public call-box at Saxton village post office, the Doctor's telephone being dead, apparently having been cut. He found the old man at home, but on the sick list with a nurse looking after him. She's been with him for some time acting as general housekeeper. It was arranged for Anna to stay there. So far so good. Ginger discovered the house was being watched – he didn't know by whom but assumed it to be by one or two of Karkoff's gang. This knocked him all of a heap. He couldn't imagine how the Doctor had been traced.'

'Never mind that. I think I know. What did Ginger do?'

'His first thought was to let you know the position. When he spoke to me his intention was to return to the house and hang on there until he had orders from you.'

'Otherwise there had been no trouble?'

'Not up to the time he was speaking. He didn't mention any.'

'So he's still there?'

'Yes.'

'Nuisance about the Doctor's phone being out of order. It means I shall have to go down. There's no other way of getting in touch with him. Is there anything here to deal with?'

'No.'

'Did you see the Air Commodore?'

'I did.'

'What were his reactions to all this?'

'He isn't happy about it. In fact, he was more than half inclined to drop the case, saying it wasn't our business. I pointed out that if we packed up now there'd be murder done as sure as fate. If we hadn't stepped in the murders would already have been done. Karkoff wouldn't be likely to pack up until he'd done what he'd been sent to do. At the finish the Chief agreed that having gone so far we might as well carry on; but at the first chance we'd better drop the case and he'd hand the whole thing over to the proper department.'

'I don't know what department he has in mind because Hampstead is already involved over the attack on Mrs Smith. But that's his worry. I'd better keep out of his way. What about you, Bertie? How did you get on?'

'No bother at all, old boy. I just whistled around until I saw no more of the Vauxhall; then I came here.'

'Where's the car?'

'I left it parked outside.'

'Good, we shall need it. Go and get the tank topped up. I'll be with you in a couple of minutes. You'd better come to Saxton with me as you've nothing else to do. I hope you won't need it but put a gun in your pocket. I'm taking one. I'm not for taking on with my bare hands people who carry knives, as we know from what happened to Agly.'

As Bertie went out Biggles turned back to Algy. 'How's your hand?'

'Not too bad.'

'Have you had it dressed?'

'Yes. The surgeon here did it.'

'Good. You hang on here where I can get you on the phone should I need more help. Let the Air Commodore know this latest development. There's a chance, too, you may have a call from Chief Superintendent Lowe who's in charge of the Mrs Smith case at Hampstead. I'll be back as soon as possible, but if the house at Saxton is being watched it means that Anna will still be in danger and I shall have to do something about it.'

'How did you get on at Hampstead?'

'Pretty well. Chief Superintendent Lowe's all right. He knows the position and has promised to co-operate. He was in a bit of a fog when I got there, stuck for a motive, which wasn't surprising. Now he has the general set-up I've left that end of the business to him. Which reminds me. Another little job you might do is ring the house agent, Mr Carson, at Hampstead, and ask him if he has had any more inquiries about Doctor Jacobs. If anyone should call he's to let us know at once.'

'Okay.'

'I'll get along. Expect me back when you see me.'

Biggles went out and joined Bertie at the car. 'Right,' he said crisply. 'Let's press on to Saxton.'

# CHAPTER 11

# GINGER TAKES CHARGE

---

Now to return to Ginger at Saxton.

As soon as he was inside the house he took Anna by the arm and said: 'Stay in. On no account go out.'

Something in his voice must have startled her. Her eyes went round. 'Not even in the garden?'

'Not one step outside the door.'

'Why?'

'Because the house is being watched. I don't know by whom but we can guess. A moment ago I saw a man lurking in the bushes. I must speak to Doctor Jacobs at once to find out if he knows anything about it.'

'He's not well.'

'What's wrong with him?'

'He's so crippled with rheumatism that he can move only with difficulty.'

'Does that mean he's confined to his bed?'

'No. Miss Johnson, the nurse, helps him to dress, and then he sits in a chair all day. She used to work with him in his surgery.'

'Have you told him what has happened, why you have come here?'

'Yes. I have told him everything.'

127

'What did he say to that?'

'He is alarmed and says I must stay here.'

'That sounds as if he doesn't know there are prowlers in the garden.

Anna opened a door leading off the hall and took Ginger into what was clearly the drawing-room, where he was introduced to Doctor Jacobs, a frail-looking white-haired old man seated in a wheel chair near the fireplace. His legs were wrapped in a travelling-rug. A fire was burning although the day was warm.

Ginger wasted no time coming to the point. 'I hope you won't think I'm being too abrupt, sir, but there is a question I must ask you at once. Anna tells me she has explained the situation. Do you know there's a man outside, watching the house from the bushes?'

The Doctor looked startled, and agitated. 'No, I was unaware of that. When I came here I did my utmost to keep my address secret, always being afraid I might have unwelcome visitors. I have taken such precautions against interference as are possible.'

'Why should *you* be afraid?'

'A man who has been concerned with political events in Germany must always be a little fearful. I knew one day I would have to write letters, and a letter can be intercepted. I wrote a letter recently to Anna's father. It might well have fallen into wrong hands had you not brought it to England.'

'Have you any idea of how anyone in Germany, apart from Anna who opened your letter, could have traced you to this address?'

'None whatever.'

'Have you written to anyone else in Berlin?'

'No.'

'Do you never receive a letter?'

'I couldn't quite say that. On occasion I have had bills from local tradesmen, who of course know I live here, although they are usually paid at the door. That cannot be prevented. The only other mail I have received since I came here is the monthly journal from the professional society of which I am a member. That comes from London.'

'So you might have been traced through the Society.'

'That is possible. The thought has never occurred to me.'

'Do you know of any man who has a right to be in the garden?'

'No.'

'You haven't a gardener – an outside man?'

'No. I used to have a gardener but I couldn't afford to keep him on.'

Ginger shook his head. 'How it has happened I can't imagine, but from the behaviour of the man I saw outside I'm pretty certain your house is being watched. The man I saw in the bushes must have been here when we arrived. I'm prepared to swear we were not followed. The reason why you're under surveillance is fairly obvious, of course. It's the same one that took these enemy agents to Hampstead. Did you by any chance send the Roths your new address, in the same way that you wrote to Professor Lowenhardt?'

'No. I never knew the Roths.'

'But you knew Professor Lowenhardt. He could have told them. Anna did, in fact, give the Roths your address, but at the time she didn't know you had moved. Naturally, when the spies discovered you were no longer at Hampstead they would concentrate on finding out where you had gone. It begins to look as if they've succeeded. My Chief sent Anna here thinking she would be

T–E

safe, but she may have jumped out of the frying-pan into the fire. I must tell him at once what has happened. May I use your telephone?'

The nurse spoke. 'I'm sorry, but it's out of order.'

Ginger frowned. 'Since when?'

'I discovered it this morning when I went to phone a tradesman in the village for some groceries. I can't get a sound out of it, which is a nuisance because it means I shall have to go to the shop. However, I have a bicycle.'

'Has this ever happened before?' asked Ginger.

'Never.'

'Strange that it should have happened at this moment, just when it is most needed. Or is it strange? I wonder.'

The Doctor had obviously not lost his faculties, for he said quietly: 'You suspect the line may have been cut?'

'That *could* be the answer. We shan't know it for certain until the breakdown has been reported. Where is the nearest telephone,'

'There's a public call-box outside the village shop, which is also the post office,' volunteered the nurse.

'I shall have to go to it right away.'

'It won't take long in the car,' said Anna.

Ginger looked at her. 'I shan't take the car.'

'Why not?'

'If I leave here alone in the car the man outside will know you are still in the house, presumably intending to stay. I'd rather he didn't know that.'

'I could go with you and come back here.'

'I don't like that idea, either. Don't forget the car we saw on the road. I'm staying here until my Chief arrives. He'll decide what's to be done about this. No. I'd rather go to the village without being seen to leave the house. With the car outside it will be supposed I'm still inside.' Ginger looked at the nurse. 'What's at the back of the house?'

'At the bottom of the vegetable garden there's a hedge. Beyond it is farm land, mostly grass fields.'

'That's the way I'll go,' decided Ginger. 'The village is no great distance so I shouldn't be away long.'

'And when you come back?' queried the Doctor.

'With your permission I shall wait here for orders.'

'Very well. I must leave it to you to do whatever you think best. As you see, I'm practically helpless.'

'Will you show me the way out of the back door?' Ginger asked the nurse. 'Anna, you stay here with the Doctor till I come back.'

The nurse took him to the rear of the house and let him out. 'Keep this door locked,' he warned her, and went on down a path between rows of vegetables. Reaching the hedge that marked the boundary he stood still for a minute to listen and survey the scene. All was quiet. Seeing nothing to cause him uneasiness he found a gap in the hedge and so reached a field where some cows were grazing. He was tempted to do some scouting in the direction of the road to see if the suspicious car was still there but decided that could wait. The road was less than a hundred yards away, as he could see from the telegraph poles that followed it, and he set off keeping more or less parallel with it. A two-decker bus heading towards the village was reassuring. He could not actually see the village as it lay in a slight hollow, but the church tower rose above it to give him the direction.

He had no trouble in reaching his objective. He didn't expect any. The phone-box was disengaged. He had to go into the shop to get some change to pay for the call.

This done he went into the box and put through a trunk call to Scotland Yard. The switchboard operator connected him with the Air Police office where, to his great satisfaction, he was answered by Algy. He had been afraid there might be no one there. He asked for Biggles, but Algy told him he had not yet returned from Hampstead. He thought he could get in touch with him there. Failing that he would give him a message as soon as he came in, which might be any minute.

Whereupon Ginger explained the situation and concluded by saying he would wait at Doctor Jacobs' house until he received instructions, which would have to be in person as the phone was out of order. That was all. Much relieved at having been able to pass his information to the office, confident that Biggles would be along as quickly as he could get to Saxton, he stepped out of the phone-box just as a car drew up outside it.

It was the Triumph he had noted parked near the Old Hall.

There was only one man in it, the driver. He got out quickly and took a pace towards the phone-box, obviously intending to occupy it. In doing this he came face to face with Ginger, as was inevitable. Recognition must have been mutual, for the man was the one who had followed him from Berlin. He was also the man, now recognisable by the material of his suit, who had put his head under the bonnet of the car when it had been parked near the entrance to the Hall.

Ginger was almost caught on one foot, as the saying is, but accustomed to shocks he didn't turn a hair. His face as they passed each other might have been that of a statue.

It was the other man who half paused in his stride and gave a slight start of surprise; and Ginger knew why. He had not seen Ginger come out of the Hall drive so he must have wondered how he had got to the village. Ginger did not enlighten him. All he wanted to know was if the man intended using the telephone. If that was his purpose it would probably be to report Anna's arrival. Wherefore he turned aside and went into the shop where he made a business of buying some cigarettes, taking as long over it as possible by chatting with the woman in charge. Through the window he saw the man go into the phone-box, make a call that lasted two or three minutes, then get back into his car and drive off, back the way he had come, in the direction of the Hall.

Ginger left the shop and looked up the road. There was no traffic, the Triumph already being out of sight, presumably on its way to resume its position near the gate. There was one pedestrian, a stoutly-built man going the same way. Ginger did not know him. He had seen him enter and leave the shop as he had gone into the phone-box.

Ginger set off back the way he had come, breaking into a trot as soon as he had left the road, by climbing over a convenient gate. It struck him that it might be a good thing to check if the car had in fact stopped. Now that he had reported to the office he could afford to take a chance to find out. With this object in view, just before reaching the vegetable garden he climbed a fence and struck off on a course which would take him a roundabout way to the back of the shrubs that lined the drive. Reaching them he steadied his pace and advanced with caution, for on his left now were the laurels in which he had seen the face of the man watching the house. With him he was not for the moment concerned, and he continued on, looking for a place that offered a view of the main road.

He stopped short when to his ears came the sound of quick footsteps on the gravel drive. They ended abruptly and at once came voices talking urgently but in tones too low for him to catch the words. Now what? he thought, trying to work it out. He made a reasonable guess at what was happening. The man in the Triumph had come to tell the watcher in the bushes that he had seen him in the village, using the telephone. So there were two of them, pondered Ginger. It was something to know that.

That was really all he wanted to know; at any rate, it was as much information as he could hope to gather in the present circumstances. There was nothing he could do to prevent the men from keeping watch on the house. They were at the moment trespassing on the Doctor's property, but there was no point in ordering them off knowing they would return as soon as he had gone. Apart from that it might start an argument that could end in violence. The time had not come for a showdown. It was sufficient to know they were there. Biggles would know how to deal with the situation when he arrived.

He was backing away intending to re-enter the house by the back door when he heard more footsteps coming up the drive. The fact that they were approaching, not receding, told him they were not being made by the man in charge of the car, returning to it. Ginger stopped. Did this mean there were three of them? If so, they were certainly concentrating on the house in force. That suggested alarming possibilities.

A sudden outcry banished all such thoughts. He stiffened, and decided quickly that this was something he could not ignore. Someone, he could not imagine who, was in trouble. It was obviously not a friend of the men already there so it followed it must be somebody on his own side. Abandoning caution he thrust his way through the bushes regardless and reached the drive to see two men, one of whom he knew by sight, holding a third. He was the stout man he had seen come out of the shop in the village. Ginger had not the remotest idea who he was, but he was not prepared to stand by and watch two men rough-handling a man much older than themselves.

'What's the idea?' he snarled, getting between the aggressors and their victim, using his hands with some force to get them apart. Taking advantage of their surprise he went on: 'I'm a police officer. Get out, you two ruffians, or I'll clap you in gaol for assault.' To the other man he said: 'Were you going to the house?'

'Yes.'

'Then go and wait for me there.'

The man hurried on without looking back.

The other two would have followed but Ginger barred their way. For a few seconds the situation looked ugly. Ginger rapped out: 'You heard what I said. Clear off and don't come back. I know who you are and why you're here. Any more trouble from you and you'll find yourselves under lock and key for illegal entry into the country.'

This may have been bluff but the threat went home. The two men hesitated, looking at each other. One said something in a low voice. He spoke quickly and in German so Ginger didn't catch the words. Anyway, they turned and walked towards the gate.

Ginger breathed a sigh of relief, for he was in no state to take on two men who would almost certainly carry weapons. He watched them until they had passed out of sight and then walked sharply to the house to see a spectacle which really did astonish him. The door was open. Standing just inside the hall was Anna and the man he had just rescued, their arms round each other.

'What's all this?' asked Ginger as he strode up looking bewildered.

'This is my father,' said Anna, with tears in her eyes. 'Isn't it wonderful?'

'For you I suppose it is,' replied Ginger, trying to keep pace with the situation.

'I'm much obliged to you, sir,' said Professor Lowenhardt.

'Don't mention it,' murmured Ginger. 'Let's get inside and shut the door. It may be too early for congratulations.'

# CHAPTER 12

# BIGGLES PLANS ACTION

To say that Ginger was shaken by the arrival of Professor Lowenhardt would hardly express his feelings. How the Professor had found his way to Saxton, or rather, how he had learned Doctor Jacobs' new address, as obviously he had, was beyond his comprehension. It was a development he could not have imagined. However, he was glad because it meant there would be one problem fewer to solve.

He had to wait until reunion with Doctor Jacobs had been effected, and Anna had explained the present situation, which took some time because the Professor knew nothing of the letter which Ginger had brought from Berlin, before he could put the question that was worrying him.

'How did you get here?' he asked.

'By train to Flaxham and then the bus,' he was told. 'I didn't know where the house was so I went to the shop to inquire the way.'

Ginger remembered seeing the bus on the road. 'I was at the phone-box when you were at the shop, but of course I didn't know who you were. What I really meant was, how did you get Doctor Jacob's address? I know you went to his old place at Hampstead because a friend of mine was there when you were attacked. You realised you'd been followed?'

'I realised it then.'

'Did you go back?'

'No. I thought I'd better keep away. My chief worry was for Anna. The morning after the attack I waited at the corner of the road hoping the postman would deliver a message for me at the house where I still supposed Doctor Jacobs was living. As it happened the milkman came along first, so I spoke to him. He shocked me by saying that the Doctor had left the house months ago and he didn't know where he had gone. I was at my wit's end. I went to the post office. They couldn't help me. Thinking about it I could see only one chance left. Knowing the Doctor was a Licentiate of Dental Surgery I went to their headquarters where they were kind enough to tell me what I wanted to know. I came here as quickly as I could, not suspecting I was still being followed.'

'You weren't,' said Ginger. 'The men who stopped you outside were already here. I can only imagine they got the Doctor's new address in the same way that you did. Spies have a way of working these things out; which, of course, is why they are spies. Unfortunately it seems that the Roths didn't think of it or they would have come here.'

'You don't know where they are, or where they might have gone?'

'No idea. We haven't a clue. Nor, apparently, have these agents who are hunting for them. But don't worry. We shall find them. It's only a matter of time.'

'What I can't understand is why I should be attacked,' said the Professor looking puzzled. 'As far as I know these spies have nothing against me.'

'I think the answer to that is fairly clear. I doubt if they have anything against you personally. Had they simply wanted to kill you they could have done that as you came up the drive. If it comes to that they could have knifed you outside the Doctor's old house at Hampstead. They wanted you alive, intending to force you to tell them where the Roths were living. You put the Roths up in Berlin, so it would naturally be assumed you knew where they had gone. In fact you did know – or thought you knew. It's the Roths they really want, not you.'

'But why do they want them? They murdered poor Hans Roth, calling it judicial execution. Isn't that enough?'

'Obviously not.'

'Why?'

'Because if my information is correct, Hans Roth, suspecting what might happen to him, made provision for it; which was a foolish thing to do because it put the lives of his family in jeopardy. He kept some important papers which the East German authorities are so anxious to get back that they're prepared to commit more murders to get them. Moritz Roth brought those papers to England with him.'

'How do you know that?'

'Anna told me.'

'If Moritz gave up the papers do you think the Roths would be left in peace?'

'You should know the answer to that better than me. I would say no, the reason being that Moritz may have read the papers and know what they contain. It's possible he has memorised them. His enemies wouldn't risk that. Even if they got the papers they wouldn't feel safe unless he was silenced.'

'I understand you are a police officer.'

'That is correct.'

'Then perhaps you can tell me what is going to happen next; what is the best thing for us to do?'

'All I can do is wait to hear what my Chief has to say about it. He should be here soon.'

'After this we shall never dare to go back to Berlin.'

'That will be a matter for you to decide. Our concern is to prevent murder being done here. From what I read in the newspapers a lot of people are in the same predicament as you are. I agree it's awful but the position might have been worse. You and Anna are together and in view of what might have happened you should be thankful for that. Had we not taken a hand things might have been very different.'

'Yes, I see that, and I am grateful; but naturally I am thinking of the future,' said the Professor earnestly. 'Expecting to be away only for a few days I brought little money with me. When I learned what Anna had done I didn't even stop to go to the bank.'

'What did you bring with you?'

'A suitcase with a change of clothes.'

'Where is it?'

'In the little hotel where I slept.'

'We'll see about that when my Chief gets here.'

'Can nothing be done with these villains who attacked me?'

'Perhaps. Up to now it has been difficult, but presently they may go too far and give us an excuse to arrest them. Our big difficulty is to find the Roths and make arrangements for their safety. That may take days.'

This somewhat profitless conversation continued into the late afternoon when the sound of a car took Ginger to a window that overlooked the front. It was the police car. Biggles and Bertie were getting out. He went to the door and let them in. He fired a question as he did so. 'Did you see a car outside on the road?'

Biggles answered. 'Yes.'

'So they're still hanging about.'

'Who?'

'One of them is the fellow who followed me from Berlin. By the way, you'll be interested to know Anna's father is here.'

'*What!*' Biggles stared. 'Where did he pop up from? What sort of lunatic game is this?'

'He got this address from some dental society. He was attacked in the drive when he arrived but I happened to be outside and took a hand.'

'Where is he?'

'With Anna. They're both with Doctor Jacobs. He's in a wheel chair helpless with rheumatism. They're all in a flap about what they're to do.'

'I'm not surprised. I'd like to know what we're going to do. I'm getting a bit tired of this hide-and-seek frolic. It doesn't seem to be getting us anywhere. Algy says the Air Commodore's getting a bit bored with it, too.'

'We can't just walk out on these wretched people and leave them to face these butchers alone.'

'I have no intention of doing anything of the sort,' returned Biggles grimly.

'What I'm wondering is, now it's known the Lowenhardts are here, will it be safe to leave them? Karkoff may suppose the Roths are here, too. He may break into the house.'

'He'll soon have to do something or he'll get a rap from the people who sent him here. He must be getting desperate and prepared to try anything. Of course, the key to the situation is the Roths. I didn't want to bring

the entire police force into this but it begins to look as if
our only chance of finding the Roths is to ask for a
general call to be put out. Our only excuse for that is
these documents Moritz is supposed to be carrying. Our
people may be glad to have a sight of them. The big snag
about staying here without a phone is we're out of touch
with the office. With these thugs outside the house is
practically in a state of siege. On the other hand we can't
stay here indefinitely. If only the gang would do something to give us an excuse to pick 'em up . . .'

Bertie spoke – the conversation still going on in the
hall. 'Would it be better to take Anna and her father
back to London?'

'I can't see how they'd be better off. With that car
outside we'd almost certainly be followed. I wonder if
it's still there. But instead of nattering here I'd better go
and have a word with Jacobs and the others. While I'm
doing that, Bertie, you might have a scout round to see if
that car is still there and how many people there are
with it. Don't start any trouble if you can avoid it.'

'Okay, old boy. Let us do a spot of hunting for a
change. I'm getting browned off with being chased
around as if we were the bally criminals.' Bertie went
out.

Ginger took Biggles into the room where everyone
was still waiting and introduced him.

'Let's see if we can get this sorted out,' said Biggles
cheerfully.

There is no need to relate in detail the debate that
followed because it did not lead to anything conclusive,
Biggles being forced to admit that he was in a quandary
as to what to do for the best. He would like a little time
to think things over.

Bertie came in. 'The car's still there,' he reported.

'Two cars, in fact. There are three men. One of them is Karkoff. Looks as if he's just arrived. The cars are together and the three of them were standing on the verge, talking, when I came away.'

'The man I saw in the village using the phone must have spoken to Karkoff. That's why he's rolled up,' surmised Ginger.

'That's about it,' agreed Biggles. 'He must have some scheme in view or there would have been no reason for him to come here.' He turned to the others present and went on. 'Will you excuse us for a few minutes while we have a conference?' He returned to the hall, Bertie and Ginger following.

'The position we have arrived at, as I see it, is this,' he stated when they were alone. 'We have two or three courses open to us. We can stay here to make sure none of these people come to any harm. The argument against that is, if nothing happened we should still be in exactly the same situation tomorrow – and the next day and the next. There's a limit to how long we can remain here doing nothing.'

'You say, if nothing happened,' put in Bertie. 'What *could* happen?'

'Karkoff and his gang might try forcing their way into the house. They can't afford to waste time any more than we can. If they tried anything like that we'd have 'em where we want 'em.'

Ginger shook his head. 'I can't see 'em being so daft as to try that knowing we were in the house. They'd know from the cars that we were still here.'

'It's a poor chance, I agree,' conceded Biggles. 'What else can we do? One thing we can't do is pull out leaving these helpless people to fend for themselves. If anything happened to them we'd never forgive ourselves. The alternative seems to be a compromise. What I mean by that is, Bertie can go back to the Yard in the Jag and report the position. Ginger goes with him, but only so far. The enemy will assume you've both gone home leaving me here on my own; they may think they can handle me and try something. Actually, Ginger will still be here, having dropped off the car as soon as it's clear and made his way back, without being seen, via the vegetable garden. Then, if any attempt is made to break into the house we should be able to grab some, if not all of them.'

'You really think they'll come?' queried Bertie.

'I can't see them sitting by the roadside all night twiddling their thumbs. They'll soon have to try something. They've less time to waste than we have. The whole thing probably depends on whether or not they believe the Roths to be here. Doctor Jacobs is here, the Lowenhardts have come here, so why not the Roths? If they decide the Roths are here – well, they'll never have a better chance to get them than in a lonely country house such as this.'

'But just a minute, old boy,' resumed Bertie. 'About this house-breaking lark. You say you think they'll try to get in. They realize the place will be locked up. It seems to me that if they have any idea of breaking in they must have brought tools with them. Surely that's enough for us? Why wait for them to burgle the place? Why not go out and search the cars? If we find suspicious tools we could pick 'em up on a charge of loitering with intent to commit a felony. If we find guns on them so much the better. We ask to see their permits. It's a million to one against them having firearm certificates. That should keep 'em in custody long enough for us to find the Roths.'

'What you're suggesting is a show-down.'

'It's about time we had one.'

Biggles drew deeply on the cigarette he had lighted. 'I think you may have something there, Bertie. There are risks. If there is anything suspicious in either of their cars they'd object to us searching them. That could only end in a scramble. On the other hand, if we found nothing we'd look silly.'

'So what?' inquired Ginger. 'What could they do about it? They'd hardly dare to make a complaint against us for unjustifiable interference. They're not even British subjects.'

'True enough. I can't see them doing that. It would suit us if they did.'

'Then we've nothing to lose and something to gain by having a crack at 'em.'

'I'm all for having a bash,' declared Bertie. 'This being given the run-around by a bunch of foreign thugs is getting under my skin.'

After considering the proposal Biggles said: 'All right. If we fail to get what we want it'll let 'em see we mean business. It's time we shook them up. It'd be something if they cleared off. That would give Anna and her father time to decide whether to stay here or look for fresh accommodation.'

'If we're going to do anything let's get on with it, while there's enough daylight to see what we're doing,' urged Ginger. 'It'll be getting dark presently.'

'We'd better tell the Doctor and the Lowenhardts what we're going to do in case the plan comes unstuck,' said Biggles. 'They could then take such precautions as would be necessary. Go and tell them, Ginger.'

Ginger obeyed. He was back inside five minutes.

'Okay,' he announced. 'I've given them the gen. It's put them in a bit of a flap.'

'They'll have to get over it,' asserted Biggles. 'Let's get on with it.'

He opened the door and had taken a pace outside when a car came tearing up the drive at a speed that made him snatch out his gun, apparently under the impression that this was a frontal attack. He returned it to his pocket as the car came to a skidding stop beside the Jaguar and the driver leapt out.

It was Algy.

'What the devil are you doing here?' snapped Biggles, looking anything but pleased.

'You'd never guess,' returned Algy. 'Hold your fire and I'll tell you.'

'I can't wait to hear.' said Biggles shortly. 'Come inside.'

# CHAPTER 13

# THE SHOW-DOWN

THEY retired into the hall.

'Now, what's all this about?' demanded Biggles.

'I've brought news, and when you've heard it you'll be glad I brought it,' stated Algy. 'I had to come myself. There was no other way I could let you know. This being out of touch is a curse. I daren't rely on a tele-gram. It might have taken hours to reach you. A phone here would have saved me a journey.'

'Okay. So you're here. Cut the cackle and let's have this news,' requested Biggles.

'It'll kill you when you hear it,' promised Algy. 'Here are the main facts. Chief Superintendent Lowe rang me at the Yard. He asked for you, of course. I told him you weren't there but I could get a message to you. This is it. He found finger-prints on the door of the house in Bishop's Way. Mrs Smith has recovered consciousness and made a statement. She said she could identify the two men who knocked her out. She saw them clearly when, hearing a noise, she came downstairs and switched on the light. That was when they went for her. She doesn't remember any more.'

'So what did Lowe do?'

'Remembering what you said about the gang staying at the hotel in Kensington he decided to arrest them on suspicion and hold them pending an identification parade. There were three of them in Karkoff's room. He got Molsk and Rallensky but Karkoff pulled a gun and shot his way out, wounding a constable. He then got away in a car. Lowe got the number and a general call has gone out to all stations to get it.'

'Did you tell Lowe where I was?'

'Of course. I also told him that some of the gang were here, or had been here. He said as soon as he could get away he'd dash down and have a word with you. He thought Karkoff might head this way to join his men here and perhaps pick them up.'

'He was right,' informed Biggles. 'Karkoff's here. At all events he was here, on the road, a little while ago, talking to the two men who had been watching the house. We were just going out to search their cars when you rolled up. Now we know how things stand we'd better get on with it. We'll grab Karkoff, anyway. Is that all?'

'Far from it. Hold your hat because this is going to rock you. The Roths have turned up. All three of them.'

Biggles stared incredulously. '*What!* Turned up? How? Where?'

'Ha! It was too simple. They've never left Hampstead. They thought Doctor Jacobs must still be there, somewhere. As they were running short of money, in desperation they did the most natural thing. They went to the police station to ask how they could get Jacobs' address. Lowe saw them himself.'

'Where are they now?'

'I don't know. Lowe said he was taking care of them until he could hand them over to you. He reckoned you'd make arrangements for them to meet Jacobs and the Lowenhardts. That's one of the reasons why he wants to see you.'

Biggles looked at the others with a queer expression on his face. 'Can you beat that? But we'd better not waste any more time talking. Thanks, Algy. Let's get after Karkoff. Resisting arrest and shooting a constable should put him out of the murder business for quite some time. Ginger, slip in and let the Lowenhardts know the Roths are safe. It'll relieve their minds to know that. Better ask Doctor Jacobs will it be all right if we bring them here. Make it snappy.'

'Are we going to walk out to the road or take one of the cars?' asked Algy while they waited for Ginger to come back.

'I'll walk, taking Bertie with me, when we've confirmed they're still there. You and Ginger follow in one of the police cars. We may need it. Okay, let's get cracking. Come on, Bertie. We'll go along the back of the bushes and jump 'em from behind the hedge. Mind how you go. Don't forget Karkoff has a gun, and having used it once against a police officer will no doubt be prepared to use it again.'

'Why do you suppose he came here?' asked Bertie, as they set off. 'I'd have thought his one idea now would be to get away. He must know a hue and cry is out for him.'

'He may have come to pick up his men, or, what's more likely, make a last attempt to get the Roths, supposing them to be here. As for getting away, where can he go? If he returns home to report failure he's had it. The people who sent him here are not the sort to forgive blunders.'

Nothing more was said, for by this time they were nearing the hedge beyond which was the road. They approached it warily. A murmur of voices reached their ears and told them what they wanted to know. Biggles beckoned and moved along the hedge a little way to a gate.

'When we're over move fast,' he whispered to Bertie. 'If they try to get away in a car shoot at a tyre.'

Bertie nodded.

Biggles took a pace forward and peeped round the end of the hedge. 'They're all there,' he breathed.

At the same time from the direction of the house came the sound of a car being started.

'Right,' said Biggles. 'This is it.' He vaulted over the gate and with Bertie by his side strode purposefully towards the cars half on the grass verge, on the opposite side of the road a dozen yards away. They were not seen for a moment, but they were heard as soon as their shoes were on the hard road surface.

Three heads turned sharply in their direction.

Biggles kept on walking. 'We're police officers and you're under arrest,' he announced in a brittle voice.

At the same time the police car swung out of the drive and pulled up beside the two vehicles already there. Algy and Ginger sprang out.

But the men on the verge were not standing still. Karkoff had a pistol out in a flash and ducking behind his car snapped a shot at Bertie who had dashed forward to prevent him from getting into it. Bertie stumbled, obviously hit, and half fell against the bonnet, clutching at it to prevent himself from falling. Before Karkoff could fire again Biggles had tackled him from behind. Locked together they fell, Biggles hanging on to the wrist of the hand that held the pistol.

Algy and Ginger could do nothing to help him. They were grappling with the other two men as they fought

furiously to get into their car, one of them using a re-
volver as a club. He managed to tear himself free and
scrambled into the driving-seat, whereupon Ginger,
with whom he had been fighting, pulled out his gun and
fired two shots into the nearest tyre.

Bertie had recovered sufficiently to go forward to
help Biggles, who was now underneath Karkoff and
having a bad time as he had to keep one hand employed
to prevent Karkoff's gun from pointing at him. Bertie
forced Karkoff's arm down, and kneeling on it wrenched
the gun free. It fell on the grass. But Karkoff, a power-
fully built man, was not finished. Still fighting like a
maniac he managed to get to his feet, and hurling Bertie
aside with a sweep of his arm made a dive for the front
seat of his car. Bertie snatched up the fallen gun but
daren't use it for fear of hitting Biggles.

Actually, at that moment, Biggles, who had drawn his
automatic, could have shot Karkoff, but, still hoping to
avoid serious casualties and feeling confident the man
couldn't get away, he refrained. A moment later, when
the opportunity had passed through Bertie getting in the
way, he wished he had not been so particular; for Bertie,
trying to grab Karkoff's legs as the man slid along into
the driving-seat, got a kick in the stomach that sent him
reeling backwards.

Karkoff, still not properly in his seat, his body lying
across both seats, reached for the starter. The engine
came to life. The car, with the door still wide open,
began to move, and Biggles had to sidestep smartly to
prevent it from knocking him down. He began shooting
at the near front tyre, but the car did not stop. He saw
Karkoff get into an upright position, and afraid he was
going to lose his man after all took a shot at him; but it
appeared to have no effect.

At this juncture, with everything in a state of wild confusion, there came a scream of brakes and skidding tyres as a black police car jerked to a stop. The near window was down. Biggles got a glimpse of the face of Chief Superintendent Lowe. He pointed at the retreating car. 'After him! It's Karkoff,' he yelled, and then, breathing heavily from his exertions stood back to watch.

It was at once evident from the way Karkoff's car was behaving that there was something wrong with it, or the driver. It looked lopsided and was swerving from one side of the road to the other. Biggles, who had not been sure that he had punctured the tyre, decided that he had. At all events it was plain that Karkoff would be overtaken by the police car, now rapidly overhauling it.

It never came to that. Karkoff was obviously having increasing difficulty in keeping his car on the road. Its swerves became wider. It then appeared as if the near wheel had seized up, for it spun off the road, crashing against a telegraph pole snapping it off, and overturned. The pole, dragging a tangle of wires with it, fell across the car. The police car skidded to a stop beside it and Lowe, with two police officers, jumped out.

Realising that was the end Biggles now looked round to see what was happening, or had happened, nearer to him. The first person his eyes fell on was Bertie, white faced, sitting on the grass holding up his left arm. There was blood on his hand. Algy was hurrying to his assistance. Beside the other car, his collar torn off and one eye closed, Ginger was holding the two men covered with an automatic. One of the men was trying to stop a bleeding nose with his handkerchief; the other sat on the running-board his face in his hands. Everyone showed signs of the conflict.

Looking worried Biggles went to Bertie. 'Are you badly hurt, old lad?'

'No. It's nothing. Got one in the top of my arm or the shoulder, I'm not sure which.'

'I'll just have a word with Lowe and we'll have a look at it,' said Biggles. 'The nurse at the house can put on a first-aid dressing and then we'll get you to hospital.'

The Superintendent came striding up the road. 'Where's the nearest telephone.'

'In the village,' answered Biggles.

'Is there a garage?'

'I don't think so. What's wrong?'

The Super came nearer. 'Did you say it was Karkoff in that car?'

'Yes.'

'Well, he won't give us any more trouble. The pole's brought the roof down and it's lying right across him. We can't shift it. It'll need a crane. We shall have to find a garage with a breakdown truck. Everything all right here?'

'More or less. They used their guns. One of my chaps is wounded. I shall have to get him to hospital.'

'Want to use my car?'

'No thanks. We've a spare car. This one that belonged to the crooks has got a flat tyre. There's one thing I wish you'd do. Take these two birds off our hands. They're two more of Karkoff's lot. I can't do anything with them.'

The Superintendent whistled down the road. The police car turned and came back. The two constables got out. 'Put the bracelets on these two,' ordered the Super.

'Good,' said Biggles. 'I'll leave you to clear up the mess. Where are the Roths?'

'At my headquarters, waiting for you.'

'Fine. I'll fetch 'em and bring 'em here as soon as I can.'

'Right! See you later.' The Superintendent turned away.

Biggles spoke to Algy and Ginger. 'Lend a hand to get Bertie into the car. We'll take him to the house. We shall have to let the Lowenhardts know what has happened.'

When they were on the way to the house Biggles went on: 'When we've had a look at Bertie's wound you two can run him to London and find him a bed in one of the hospitals. You can then collect the Roths from Hampstead and bring them here – that is if Doctor Jacobs can put them up. I'll wait for you in the house.'

This all worked out as planned.

The Lowenhardts looked horrified when Bertie was helped in, but the nurse, when she had been told what had happened, got busy.

Bertie was made comfortable on a couch. His jacket, bloodstained shirt and vest were removed and the wound examined. It was nasty, but no worse than had been expected. Fortunately the bullet hadn't touched a bone. Striking the muscle of the upper arm near the shoulder it had gone clean through. It had bled a lot, which made it look worse than it really was. Bertie, of course, made light of it, but Biggles was taking no chances and treated it seriously.

The nurse dressed and bandaged the wound with materials from Doctor Jacobs' medical equipment. Bertie was wrapped in a rug and settled in the back seat of the police car. Algy and Ginger got in and were soon on their way.

By this time it was dark. 'Take it steady,' Biggles warned them.

With the others he went back into the drawing-room.

So far, in the urgency of dealing with Bertie not a word had been said about the final outcome of the affair on the road and he now proceeded to explain what had happened.

'The first thing you'll be happy to know is, your friends the Roths will soon be on their way here,' he said.

There were expressions of surprise and joy at this.

'Where are they?' asked Anna.

'At Hampstead police headquarters. As soon as Algy and Ginger have seen Bertie safely into hospital they're bringing them here. I trust that's all right with you, sir?' Biggles looked at the Doctor.

'Of course. I am overjoyed. I have plenty of room.'

'Good. Then that settles that. They should be safe here, anyhow for a time. Karkoff, I believe, is dead, or if he isn't he soon will be. The rest of the gang are under arrest, and for shooting a police officer they're likely to be behind bars for a long time.' Biggles went on to narrate all that had happened, both in London and on the road outside. 'I'm staying here to have a word with the Roths when they come. After that I shall go back to London. I shall have to speak to you all again later, of course. You may be required to give evidence, to the police if not in court.'

'How long is it since you had anything to eat?' inquired the Doctor, practically.

Biggles smiled. 'Come to think of it, quite some time.'

'Then I hope you will join us at our evening meal. I'm afraid it will have to be a cold one.'

'Thank you,' acknowledged Biggles. 'That is an invitation I shall not decline.'

It meant a long wait, of course, before Algy and

Ginger could return, and after the meal the time was passed by Biggles recounting in more detail the events that had led to the present situation. There was still much Professor Lowenhardt did not know.

'What I do not understand is how you came into this in the first place,' said the Professor. 'Are you and your colleagues secret service agents?'

'No, but we're not quite ordinary police officers,' answered Biggles. 'As a matter of fact, and there is no reason why you shouldn't know this, we were tipped off by a German friend of ours, also a refugee from East Germany, now resident in this country, that Karkoff and his assassins were here. Events in Berlin told us the probable purpose of their visit.'

'I think the friend was Erich von Stalhein,' put in Anna.

Biggles smiled gently. 'In this country we have a saying "no names no pack drill". No doubt you'll be seeing Von Stalhein shortly, and then you can ask him about it.'

The Professor nodded sagely. 'It is a good thing not to mention names,' he agreed. 'In these unhappy days it is not easy to know who to trust.'

The conversation then moved on to what steps the visitors should take to prevent themselves from further molestation.

'It will depend to a great extent on Moritz Roth,' stated Biggles. 'He still holds the key to the situation with these documents he has brought out of Germany. I don't think Anna and the Professor have much to worry about. Their trouble has been caused by the assumption that they knew where the Roths were hiding. But I don't think there can be any question of the Roths returning to Berlin, unless . . .'

'Unless what?' asked Anna.

'Unless Moritz returns those papers he has brought away with him. I don't know what information they contain but they must be of vital importance to the people who now control East Germany or they wouldn't have gone to such lengths to recover them.'

'You think he should burn them, perhaps?'

'No. That would serve no useful purpose because it would not be known they had been destroyed. If he said so it's unlikely he would be believed.'

'Then what do you think he should do with them?'

'One plan would be to hand them over to me. I would pass them on to my Chief, and he – having had a look at them of course – could no doubt arrange for them to be sent through diplomatic channels either to the authorities in West Berlin, or direct to East Germany, which ever might be considered best. That is for us to decide. In either case the East Berlin secret police would soon know that Moritz no longer had them. They might wonder if he ever had them. Anyhow, that should remove the danger from Moritz, although that is not to say he'd be entirely safe were he to return to Germany. He might be seized for questioning. For the time being, as Doctor Jacobs has been kind enough to offer you all his hospitality you'd better stay here. I shall discuss the matter with my Chief. Let's leave it at that,' he concluded.

A car door slammed outside.

'That sounds as if your friends have arrived,' said Doctor Jacobs.

'I'll let them in,' answered Biggles. 'It's getting late so we shan't stay long; but I must have a word with Moritz.'

*       *       *

There is really little more to tell. The rest, although it occupied some time, was no more than a matter of routine work for the police. With the murder gang safe under lock and key the peril in which the refugees had stood no longer existed so they were able to relax.

Superintendent Lowe had been right about Karkoff. He was dead before he could be extricated from the crashed car. The others, his assistants, received long prison sentences on charges of breaking into the house of Mrs Smith at Hampstead and causing her 'grievous bodily harm' – to use the official wording, and for attempted murder by shooting at police officers. The fact that their passports were found to be forgeries made their case worse. Biggles had nothing to do with this as the prosecution was handled by normal police methods.

Bertie had to spend a week in hospital before being discharged fit for light duties. He considered himself lucky. As Biggles told him cheerfully, in the work they were doing this sort of thing was bound to happen occasionally. It was only on television that people could spend their lives dodging bullets without ever getting in the way of one.

Biggles had to do a lot of explaining to the Air Commodore, who suggested that in future he would be better advised to mind his own business.

The Air Commodore took over the documents which Biggles had obtained from Moritz and had nearly cost several people their lives. Moritz needed no persuasion to pass them on, being, as he said, only too glad to be rid of them. What finally became of them Biggles was not informed. As he told Von Stalhein when they met for lunch shortly afterwards, he neither knew nor cared where they went.

The Roths had the most difficult problem to face, for

after what had happened they were advised not to return to Berlin. They stayed with Doctor Jacobs for some time, indeed, until their property in Germany had been disposed of by an estate agent. This provided them with some money. The last that was heard of them was they had gone to America, where Professor Lowenhardt and Anna were to join them as soon as it could be arranged. That this had been accomplished was learned when in due course Christmas cards were received from Mr and Mrs Moritz Roth; from which it was gathered that Moritz and Anna were married.

As Biggles remarked in the office as he closed the file on the case, so they all lived happily ever after; and although it might be a bit old-fashioned there was no better ending to a tale than that.

Captain W. E. Johns wrote over eighty books about Biggles, the intrepid airman whose adventures take him and his comrades all over the world.

Many of these books are still available, published by Brockhampton Press. Here is a list of the titles available in Knight Books:

BIGGLES AND THE CHINESE PUZZLE
BIGGLES BURIES THE HATCHET
BIGGLES INVESTIGATES
BIGGLES AND THE NOBLE LORD
BIGGLES IN THE UNDERWORLD
BIGGLES AND THE DARK INTRUDER
BIGGLES AND THE BLUE MOON
BIGGLES AND THE GUNRUNNERS
BIGGLES AND THE LITTLE GREEN GOD
BIGGLES AND THE PENITENT THIEF
BIGGLES AND THE BLACK MASK
BIGGLES SORTS IT OUT
BIGGLES FLIES WEST
BIGGLES' SPECIAL CASE

Ask your local bookseller, or at your public library, for details of other Knight Books, or write to the Editor-in-Chief, Knight Books, Arlen House, Salisbury Road, Leicester LE1 7QS.